W9-BKZ-825

The Last Summer
Spain 1936

BY THE AUTHOR

Grip, a Dog Story
Running Wild
The Mysterious Appearance of Agnes
Just a Dog
Russian Blue
Moshie Cat
Stallion of the Sands
Leon
The Wild Horse of Santander
The Greyhound
The Wild Heart
Horse in the Clouds

HELEN GRIFFITHS

The Last Summer
Spain 1936

Illustrated by Victor Ambrus

HOLIDAY HOUSE · NEW YORK

© Helen Griffiths 1979
Illustrations © Hutchinson Junior Books Ltd 1979
First American publication 1979 by Holiday House, Inc.
Printed in the United States of America

Library of Congress Cataloging in Publication Data

Griffiths, Helen.
The last summer.

SUMMARY: A boy and a horse share adventures during
the Spanish Civil War.
[1. Spain—History—Civil War, 1936-1939—Fiction.
2. Horses—Fiction] I. Ambrus, Victor G. II. Title.
PZ7.G8837Las   [Fic]   79-10469
ISBN 0-8234-0361-0

131586

I

On his first afternoon at the house on his father's country estate, Eduardo lay in a shuttered, heat-battered bedroom listening to the silence. He thought he could hear the distemper on the outside wall cracking under the glare of the sun until a bluebottle, droning with almost musical cadence, interrupted his concentration. From somewhere came a clink – one short, sharp sound – and his ears strained to hear it again, hoping to identify it. It didn't come again and he sighed, stretching out his hand for the watch on the bedside table, grimacing as he calculated that he had to remain here for another half an hour at least.

Unendurable torture! No, not unendurable because he had to endure it. His father had said so.

'It will be cooler at six. You can get up then, have something to eat if you're hungry, go for a walk and then get back to your studies till half past nine.'

Go for a walk! Where could he walk to? If he were still in Madrid he could think of a dozen places, and all of them fun because he would be with his friends. But here, in the middle of nowhere and with a sun that burned right through to his bones! Was he really expected to go for a walk?

He sighed again, wondering how he would endure the ten days, perhaps longer, his father proposed to spend here.

This was the first time Eduardo had visited the estate, and the expectation with which he had started out was already quenched. There was no doubt that his father had brought him here as a punishment. Surely no one would come here for fun, unless they came as his father usually did, with a group of business friends in the hunting season, shooting all day and talking all night.

That was how his mother described what they did. She had never been to the estate either. She didn't like the country. Once she had stayed at their house in Sevilla, some sixty kilometres away, but she had been ill there all the time because of the heat. She was from the north, from a fishing town on the Galician coast where Eduardo always spent his holidays – swimming, going out with the fishermen his grandfather employed, playing games with his cousins up there and his summer friends.

If his father had brought him now for the hunting, he was sure he could have enjoyed himself here, too. In the salon at home they had the stuffed head of the big stag his father had killed a couple of years previously and there were two smaller heads in the hall. His mother detested them. She couldn't bear animals of any kind, not even dead ones, but his father liked to boast about those heads so they stayed there, along with the glass cases containing various wild birds among dried flowers and grasses. In the dining room of this house was the head of the famous boar, the subject of his father's favourite hunting story, which his mother had absolutely refused to have hung in the salon at home and which looked tatty now with neglect.

But he wasn't here for any hunting. He was here because he had failed his exams in physics and chemistry. The rest of his school report had been good, but unless he passed those two subjects when he was re-examined in September, he wouldn't be allowed to start next year's studies. To make things worse, the sons of all the people his father knew had passed their exams with honours – or so they said. None of them were having to resit any subjects or were threatened with repeating a whole year's work. Eduardo knew it was this that rankled his father more than anything else.

'I've told you more than once, I want you to be the best. You are my only son. If there were half a dozen of you, it wouldn't matter quite so much. But all my pride is in you. You have a duty not to fail me. You have a duty to bring me good results, not this!' he had exclaimed, thrusting the report under his son's nose.

Eduardo supposed that he ought to be glad that he hadn't been beaten, which was what happened to some of his friends in the same circumstances, but his father's way of crushing him hurt as deeply as any physical pain. His look was so hard, his words overwhelming. To disappoint him was unforgivable.

'I had good marks in everything else,' he had dared to defend himself, because he knew he had worked and that his teacher had been unfair.

'I hardly think a client of mine would accept as an excuse for losing his case the fact that I had won a dozen others the previous month. That's not the way of things, my boy. Excuses are for underlings. In September you are going to pass those subjects with top marks, and to make sure you do, there'll be no holiday for you until I've satisfied myself that you've been through your books from beginning to end.'

Eduardo wouldn't have minded so much had he been allowed to take his books to Galicia with him. His mother already had the train tickets. They had left Madrid every first of July for as long as he could remember, his father joining them for the rest of the summer a few weeks later. This year his father had to go to the estate and, saying that his mother would never be severe or consistent enough to make him study, decided to take him along.

'While I'm sorting out my affairs you can get down to work. It's quiet there. There'll be no distractions. And if you want to get to Galicia in August, instead of spending the whole summer in Madrid with a private tutor, you'd better show me that you do have a sense of responsibility after all.'

His mother had been against the idea.

'It's so hot there at this time of year. It's not good for him. And suppose there's trouble? You know what the talk is. Revolution . . . war. . . .'

'And it's still only talk,' was his impatient reply. He didn't like to be contradicted. 'Besides, it's only for a few days, ten at the most. Then I'll take him up to Galicia myself.'

Eduardo's mother had put up unusual resistance, in spite of his father's displeasure, sure that only in her home town and with her family would they all be safe from the growing turmoil of strikes, burnings and street warfare in Madrid. None of these things meant anything to Eduardo. There was always a lot of political talk at home because his father was a lawyer with a position in the Ministry of Justice and had friends who were important people. In the last few months especially, they had shouted and banged on the table a lot in the evenings, but Eduardo never listened to anything they said, though the words came clearly through the closed doors and echoed round most of the apartment.

His hopes that his father could be persuaded to change his mind and let him go to Galicia as planned were dashed. Only the prospect of perhaps being allowed to handle the hunting rifles lessened the intimidating dread of spending ten days alone with him. He demanded such a high standard of obedience and respect that often Eduardo felt his father was kinder to the servants than to him.

He wasn't particularly interested in seeing the estate. Had they been going to stay with his Uncle Ramon it would have been different. His uncle bred fighting bulls, good ones – he had seen them in Madrid – but his father didn't get on well with Ramon and, the house in Sevilla being rented out, preferred to stay at his own country house, with all its inconveniences, rather than accept Ramon's hospitality.

His father's five thousand acres supported no bulls and the

land was untended. It was good hunting country, half of it covering the hills of the sierra, the other half planted with olive trees allowed to run wild ever since labour troubles a few years earlier had made him vow he would give no more employment to the local people. He had no love for the land and, with his various business interests, his lawyer's practice and his position in the Ministry, needed no income from it. Inherited from his father, to him it was nothing more than a hunter's retreat and a burden. His brother, whose estate it bordered, had offered to buy it from him.

All these things he had explained to Eduardo on the long car journey through La Mancha and Córdoba, the sleek, pale blue Hispano Suiza dominating the bad roads as well as the good ones. He was serene, friendly and talkative at the wheel and Eduardo wished he was always like this.

They had arrived at nightfall on the eleventh of July, and Maruja, after recovering from her surprise, made up their beds and put away the supplies brought in the hamper which her husband, Baltasar, had carried in from the car, together with the suitcases.

In the morning, with his head full of stories of deer, wolves and wild boar, Eduardo had discovered a canary, two finches, some chickens, two greyhounds and a horse. There didn't seem to be anything else, and before he could question Baltasar, his father had called him in to his books.

'You're here to work, remember,' was his severe reminder.

So he listened to the silence in the shuttered room, remembered his friends in Madrid, thought about the cool sea of Galicia, and wondered where he could possibly go or what he could possibly see once he was allowed to get up. He decided he would go and talk to Baltasar. There was really nothing else that he could do.

2

When Eduardo went downstairs at six o'clock, he found his father in the dining room, one end of the long polished table covered with documents and buff folders tied with red ribbons. His father looked up over his glasses, which he was inclined to wear at the end of his nose when working, and pointed to the dish of smoked ham, cheese and olives that Maruja had set out for them at the other end.

'Have something to eat,' he said, 'then go and amuse yourself for a while. At seven I shall expect you to be here at the table, with your books open.'

'Are you having something?' asked Eduardo politely, sitting down in front of the shiny brown dish with its chunks of dark ham cut roughly but appetizingly.

'No, no. But you eat. I promised your mother you would eat well.'

Eduardo remembered his mother's last anxious words when they went to see her off at the station. 'Make him eat well, Manolo.' She fussed terribly about his food.

She fussed about his father, too, who ate very little considering his size. Had he not been tall he would have been fat. As it was, he was portly in an unobtrusive way, imposing in figure as well as in looks. As usual, he was making no concession to heat or circumstances, sitting there as if he were in his office in Madrid, wearing both jacket and tie and with his shirt done up to the top button, his solid silver fountain pen hovering over the long folios which engaged his attention.

Aware of his son's gaze, he looked up to say, 'You see, Eduardo, even I have to bring my work with me. Things can't be left because they're dull or difficult. They have to be tackled to the best of one's ability.'

Baltasar's wife, small, thin and sharp-eyed, dressed in black even to the apron which reached her ankles, came in with a jug of almond milk, and as soon as he had swallowed most of it Eduardo was out of the shadowy dining room and into the sunshine, screwing up his eyes as he glanced about, wondering what to do and where he would find Baltasar.

The house was built round a patio with the stables and kitchen on one side and the living quarters opposite. He had already explored the stables that morning, finding them big enough to house a dozen animals but obviously unused for years. It looked as though even Baltasar's horse never stayed there, so much did neglect lie over everything.

Baltasar and Maruja didn't live in the house, which had been entirely shut up until their arrival last night. They had a little cottage at some distance behind it, overshadowed by the eucalyptus trees that grew in a tall row beside a wide but not very deep water tank. There was a wind pump, as tall as the trees, which brought water up from the river half a kilometre away, and just beyond that was the cottage. You could hardly see its walls for the thick-leaved vine branches spreading in every direction, while the two windows were almost equally well-hidden by geraniums of every colour which stretched up behind the gratings and cascaded from tins tied to them.

As Eduardo approached he saw the man he was looking for sitting in the doorway on a low chair, a bridle across his knees, rags in his hands and near his feet. Beyond the shadows the dead-looking greyhounds soaked up the sun.

'You're called Eduardo,' Baltasar greeted him without any ceremony as soon as he was close enough. He went on, 'Like the old master, Don Eduardo, your grandfather.'

Eduardo nodded.

'And how old are you?' Even while he talked and smiled up at him, his hands went on working at the leather, the oil-soaked rags smelling strongly and not too agreeably.

'Eleven – well, nearly twelve.' It sounded better like that, though not quite true. 'What are you doing?'

'What you can see,' was the answer, and he half lifted the bridle in explanation. 'It's the old girl's. I clean it every day.'

'Why?'

'Touch it and you'll see why.'

Eduardo stepped closer to feel the bridle, more affected by the smell of the rags mingled with Baltasar's air of stale garlic than impressed by the softness of the leather between his fingers.

'Smooth as a baby's bottom,' said Baltasar proudly. 'Not a crack and as good as new. How old do you think this bridle is, eh? How old?'

Eduardo shrugged, moving out of range of the man's breath.

'Well, I can tell you. Sixteen years old. It's the oldest of them all. Her very first bridle. The señorita had it specially made for her.'

'Who?'

'The mare, of course.'

Baltasar was talking in riddles, Eduardo thought, staring at the wrinkled face with its stubble of grey whiskers which he was never to see any thicker or any shorter, as if they never grew. A stained black Andalusian hat protected his baldness from the sun. He could have been any age between fifty and seventy. To Eduardo he was just old.

'I mean, who?' he said impatiently. 'You said "the señorita".'

Baltasar looked at him in astonishment. 'Your aunt, of course. The Señorita Angeles.'

'Oh!' He had just about forgotten her. After all, she died

when he was only five or six and he'd never even met her. 'Did she live here then?'

'After Don Eduardo died and the lands were divided, she sold her share to your uncle and lived with him. But it didn't work out so she moved here. Your father never lived here, so he didn't mind.'

'I didn't know,' said Eduardo.

All the time Baltasar went on rubbing the leather, his fingers seeming to caress the different pieces as they passed over them. He stopped for a moment and stared lingeringly at the boy, taking in his wheat-coloured hair, grey eyes and pale skin.

'She looked just like you,' he said. 'She was a good-looking woman, very good looking.'

'Didn't she marry?'

The old man snorted derisively. 'Her? Marry? There was only one love in her life. She made that obvious to everyone. That's why she never got married.'

'Oh. Who did she love?'

'Well, I thought everyone knew that,' exclaimed Baltasar, getting every last ounce of interest out of his story. He didn't often have an audience for his words. His wife had stopped listening to him years ago.

'Who?' demanded Eduardo impatiently.

Baltasar jerked his head as if indicating somewhere over his shoulder, beyond the cottage.

'I bet she's watching you now, isn't she? She's a nosey old devil. Has to know everything that's happening. She knows you've never been here before.'

Eduardo looked. All he could see was the grey horse, about fifty metres away. Its head was down to the ground and it was pulling industriously at the parched grass, but it did look as if it had an eye on both of them.

Doubtfully he said, 'You mean . . . the horse?' He had a suspicion that Baltasar was pulling his leg.

'Can you see anyone else?'

'No, but how do you know she's there? You can't see her and you didn't look.'

'I don't need to look. That old lady loves me better than my wife. Where I go, she goes. Now she's curious about you, wants to know who you are and what you're doing here. We don't often have visitors, you know.'

Incredulously, Eduardo looked at the horse again. He had never really looked at any horse before and knew nothing about them. There were horses in Madrid, not many because the carts and wagons were mainly pulled by mules and donkeys and they were usually dirty, smelly things covered with flies and stale manure. However, in spite of his ignorance and disinterest, he could see that she was not to be compared with them.

To start with, she was clean. Her dark, dappled skin shone in the sunlight, and as her steel-grey tail swished across her flank, every strand of hair fell loosely, unclogged. The long, wavy forelock almost covered her eyes and her sharp ears moved constantly back and forth as, imperceptibly, she grew closer.

Eduardo turned impatiently back to the old man, certain now that he was trying to make a fool of him. 'But she's only a horse. How could my aunt be in love with a horse?'

Baltasar gazed thoughtfully at him, actually forgetting the bridle. Hope seemed to die out of his almost black eyes, then he sighed and his hands started moving again.

'Of course. If you don't know anything about horses . . .'

'And how am I supposed to know anything about horses?' demanded Eduardo, feeling that Baltasar had shut him out of his confidence, annoyed by it. He suddenly felt worthless, standing there, utterly ignored.

'Here, no one knows anything about horses,' remarked Baltasar sarcastically. 'Well, there's no one here anyway to know about anything or to care about anything. Your uncle, now, he knows about horses. He's got some fine horses but none as fine as that one.'

He jerked his head in the grey's direction again on the last words.

'She doesn't look fine to me,' replied Eduardo, wanting to taunt him, roused by the old man's unspoken accusation and the dart of scorn in his eyes. His cheeks were flushed with angry disdain. 'I thought she was yours. I thought she pulled a cart, like a donkey or mule.'

Then Eduardo discovered that Baltasar had his pride, too. He seemed to grow in the chair without moving from it and his dark eyes blazed.

'Señorito, I'd pull a cart myself before letting that mare know what a harness is. It's only your ignorance that makes you think you know so much. You'd better get back to your books. I hear that's what Don Manuel brought you here for. A wise man only talks about what he knows.'

Eduardo stalked away, smarting at the rebuke and because already everyone knew that he was in disgrace. Even if 'everyone' were only Baltasar and his wife, they still knew. Servants had a way of knowing everything.

He refused to look at the horse, even though something urged him to do so, and he wouldn't run either, although he wanted to.

'Señorito!'

The way Baltasar called made him stop and look back. There was forgiveness and apology in the tone.

'Go and see your uncle's horses,' he said. 'And then come back and look at this one.'

3

He was back in the dining room before seven and decided to make a special effort this first evening to please his father and so perhaps be allowed to spend several days at his uncle's estate which would be far more interesting than this awful place. It wasn't because of Baltasar that he wanted to go; he couldn't care less about the old man and the silly things he had said about the horse; but because he knew he had cousins there and because of the bulls. Bulls would be far more interesting to look at than horses.

His father sat with him until half past nine, glancing at him every now and then to make sure he wasn't distracted, and then Maruja began preparing the table for supper. He gave his books to his father.

'Not bad, not bad,' he commented, going through the work which had run into two pages on each subject. 'You see, you can do well when you try.'

Encouraged, he asked, 'Papa, can I go with you to Uncle Ramon's? I'll still do my work there, I promise?'

'We'll both have to go there tomorrow. Maruja has reminded me that it's the saint's day of the village and your uncle always holds a special celebration at the house as well as attending the village fiesta. If I'd thought of it before I wouldn't have come down here till next week. There won't be a chance to discuss business till it's over. As it is, we have no alternative but to attend.'

His lack of enthusiasm couldn't dampen Eduardo's spirits,

however. Although he knew very little about his father's family, his mother's ill-health having obliged him to spend a good deal of his childhood in Galicia among her people, it was sufficient for him to know that in Sevilla fiestas were very gay affairs, celebrated with bulls and flamenco, and that not even his father could stop him enjoying himself.

And so it was. The Hispano Suiza found its way along the almost impassable tracks through the hills that separated the two estates, and on their arrival at the house the brothers hugged each other, one with solemnity, the other with enthusiasm, while Eduardo eyed his cousins, all older than he was, whom he hardly remembered from a visit they had made to Madrid. There were seven of them – which was why, Ramon remarked jokingly as he re-introduced his sons and daughters to them, he needed to buy up so much land – and

they dashed about all over the place with a noisy gaiety which soon caught Eduardo in its swirl.

His Uncle Ramon was the most easy-going character he could imagine, his wife equally so, and the only persons who seemed to give any orders about the house were the servants, who scolded the master with the same ferocity they used on the children. No wonder the two brothers could hardly bear to see each other. They had absolutely nothing in common.

Eduardo forgot about chemistry and physics as he splashed in the river that crossed his uncle's land. None of his cousins thought about studying, although they had an English tutor who was learning Spanish faster than they were learning any English. They spent most of the year in various boarding schools in Switzerland and France and were wildly excited because they had just come home for the holidays; because their father had given three bulls to the villagers for the fiesta; and because the day after that there would be a display at their own private bull-ring, led by a well-known torero who would stay for a few days before going on to his engagement at Sevilla.

Although he didn't ask them to, they took him to see some of the horses. Most of them, the brood mares and young stock, were too far off to be looked at. They grazed on the plains under the watchful eyes of the herdsmen, almost as wild as the bulls, but there was a stable block with high-walled corrals where a dozen horses stood. The majority were greys, like Baltasar's mare, with black legs and either black or silvery manes and tails, Andalusians with Roman heads and intelligent eyes. There were two black stallions and a chestnut. The chestnut was pure Arab, on lease from the Army stud because Ramon was keen to improve his stock with Arab blood, and the blacks were crossbreeds, combining the best of both lines.

While Eduardo listened to all his cousins told him, he tried to picture Baltasar's old horse and compare them. In the end he gave up. To him they were just horses, magnificent creatures no doubt, their satin-like skins glistening in the sunlight and somewhat frightening with their tossing heads, nervous hooves and loudly blowing nostrils. He couldn't see any difference between these and Baltasar's, except that the grey mare was quieter, probably because she was old. What made one better than another? How did you judge a horse? He wasn't really interested enough to ask, anxious to move on to the bulls and cows penned in the corrals beyond the bull-ring.

He spent a long time looking at the three bulls which were to be herded down to the village in the cool of the evening, two three-year-olds and a seven-year-old stud bull which hadn't proved its worth.

'One of the youngsters is blind in one eye,' the most knowledgeable cousin explained, 'and the other's lost the tip off its left horn. We only give the defective ones away, of course.'

'What's wrong with the big one then?' wondered Eduardo, who could see nothing but ferocious strength and formidable power in its every movement.

'Oh, he's too big and dangerous. No professional would agree to fight him.'

In the next pen were two heifers and a rangy five-year-old cow. One heifer was for the visiting torero, the second was for the amusement of his uncle's employees, while the cow was for Ramon himself who fought on horseback.

'Why doesn't he fight a bull?' asked Eduardo.

'Because cows are much more dangerous.'

Ramon was a brilliant rider in spite of his paunch, his fat legs and double chin, as he demonstrated the day after the village fiesta when he pitched his own ability and the understanding of his favourite stallion, Azabache, against the cow's cunning, speed and blind fury. It seemed to Eduardo that the whole performance was done by magic. Did the horse move of its own accord? Did the rider tell him what he must do? He was aware of no signals, no cues, and yet the two creatures, man and horse, knew exactly what each required of the other as they danced just beyond the reach of the swiftly raking horns, charging the cow when it wouldn't come to them, escaping a terrible goring by what seemed a hair's breadth every time.

She was too good a cow to kill, one of his bravest, so eventually Ramon signalled for her to be let out of the ring, and then the stallion went down on its knees with tossing head in acknowledgement of the spectators' applause.

The days Eduardo spent at his uncle's estate were crowded with excitements of every kind, but the thing that impressed him most was that display of horsemanship. The torero was skilful in the courting and killing of his heifer but the haughty, prancing arrogance of the quivering black stallion was the most powerful thing he had seen. So what did Baltasar mean by comparing that old grey mare with Uncle Ramon's Azabache? It was something he would have to discover, if only he could find the opportunity.

As far as he could see, his uncle was beleaguered by people the whole time, with whom he cracked jokes, shared toasts, laughed and slapped on the back. As his father had foreseen, there was no hope of talking business and he wasn't likely to be interested in any comments from old Baltasar. He probably wouldn't even know which horse he was talking about.

His chance didn't come until he was back in his father's car, ready to return to the empty house and his studies, and the whole family swarmed round to say good-bye all over again, after having already said good-bye inside the house.

'Uncle Ramon,' shouted Eduardo above the noise of half a dozen voices, 'do you know Aunt Angeles' horse?'

'Aunt Angeles' horse!' Everybody was suddenly silent with surprise.

'Well, Baltasar said she belonged to her.'

'A grey with black points? A mare?'

Eduardo nodded, not sure what 'points' were but knowing they could only refer to the same animal.

'She's still alive, is she?' There was fond incredulity in his expression.

'Baltasar said she's a better horse than any of yours.'

'Did he now?'

'It isn't true, is it?'

'Baltasar knows as much about horses as I do.'

'But what about the black, Azabache? She can't be as good as that,' he insisted.

'That's one of her sons and, although I've worked on him for eight years, he'll never be as good as she was.'

The sound of the engine and the squeals of half his cousins as they heard it almost drowned Ramon's last sentence so that Eduardo couldn't really believe he had heard aright, but he couldn't ask any more because his father was getting impatient. He didn't like people leaning all over his Hispano Suiza and besides, the sun was burning down on their necks.

'I'll be back when you've recovered from the celebrations,' he shouted to his brother as the vehicle moved off, 'and then we'll do some serious talking. I've got to be back in Madrid by the twentieth so you'd better be making up your mind.'

No one who heard him say that could possibly have known that he would be dead before then. The only thing Eduardo was sure of as they bumped slowly over the cart track that had brought them there was that he would now have to go back to dreary chemistry and physics and that both Uncle Ramon and Baltasar were pulling his leg about the old horse.

Didn't his mother always say that Andalusians exaggerated more than anyone else, that you couldn't take them seriously for a moment, and that his father was only the exception that proved the rule? 'I thought he was from Galicia, too, when I first met him,' she once laughed, which for her was high praise indeed.

4

Eduardo had to study for two hours in the morning. The rest of the time was his and, because there was nothing else to do and because Uncle Ramon's mysterious remarks had aroused his curiosity, he decided to talk to Baltasar again about the old horse. But first of all he thought he would look at her by himself so that the old man couldn't accuse him again of not knowing what he was talking about. So far he had only seen her from a distance and among shadows. Perhaps a closer view would tell him more.

What surprised him was that the mare didn't seem to have a particular paddock or pasture. As far as he could see, she roamed wherever her fancy took her. There were no fences to stop her and yet she didn't run away. In fact, now that he thought of it, she always seemed to be somewhere near Baltasar.

The sun glared so hotly that he hoped he wouldn't have to go very far to find her. Yesterday she had been among the eucalyptus trees near the windmill but today she was nowhere in sight. He could have asked Baltasar but pride wouldn't let him. He didn't want the old man to think he was interested, because really he wasn't. He just had nothing else to do.

This was all such dull land compared to the green and densely wooded Galicia, with its hills and valleys and sandy estuaries. Whatever grass struggled through the dusty soil was short and dry, and there were thistles growing everywhere to great heights, uncontrolled, unheeded, their bright, purple flowers in startling contrast with the lustreless green of the neglected olive trees and the ochre-red earth. Stiff blue flowers grew in patches on spikey stalks, and here and there was the blood-red splash of a solitary poppy. The blues and reds and purples were as harsh and glaring as the sun.

Maruja, coming from the cottage, saw him wandering about and sent him down to the river, at the bottom of a hill covered with olive trees. As he went through them he caught the flash of sun on water and a patch of green, unbelievably brilliant. Soon he saw Baltasar and the mare. She was eating from his hands. The old man saw him and waved, making the mare throw up her head. She saw him too, and Eduardo noticed how her ears strained in his direction, bits of green stuff hanging from her jaws forgotten.

'So you've come to see her at last,' called Baltasar as he approached. 'Now you know I didn't lie to you, eh?'

Conceited old man, thought Eduardo. As if he even cared!

He stopped a few yards away, not sure about drawing too close to the mare who from this short distance suddenly looked very large and imposing. Her eyes, big and dark and with deep hollows above, were full of questioning and he could sense the stiff alertness in which her whole body was held. As he didn't know whether she was going to attack him or run away, he was very cautious about getting nearer to her.

'That's it,' said Baltasar softly. 'Just stand there and let her look at you. Once she knows you she'll make friends if you let her – and if she likes you.'

'If she likes me!'

Baltasar's last words struck him oddly but he stood there anyway, uncomfortable under the curious animal gaze but not wishing to show it, wanting to prove to himself also that he wasn't afraid of her. But Baltasar knew.

'Relax,' he suggested. 'She won't hurt you.'

The truth was that Eduardo had never been so close to any animal before. He had never had a dog sniff at him and he had never felt any warm, live body under his hand. He hadn't dared to touch his uncle's horses and hadn't been as close to them as this. The mare was so near that he could smell her. It wasn't a bad smell really; warm, earthy, a bit sweet.

He started and involuntarily stepped back a pace as she suddenly stretched forward her head to push her black muzzle against him.

'Give her a pat on the neck,' encouraged Baltasar. 'Show her you're friendly.'

But Eduardo wasn't prepared to go so far just yet. He stood his ground, however, and let her sniff him, and she left a green smudge on his clean shirt, making him jump back with annoyance. She lost interest in him and turned to Baltasar again whose hands were full of the lush alfalfa that grew along the river bank behind the only fence Eduardo had yet seen. It wasn't a very good fence, made up of broken boughs and thorn bushes, an old iron bedstead and what looked like cartwheels and planks, makeshift but enduring.

She tugged the long green strands from Baltasar's hands, munching loudly even while her black lips anxiously gathered the next mouthful. The man teased her a little, not letting go of the stems or pulling them out of her reach, and she stamped a hoof impatiently, upper lip stretching and twisting like rubber, making Eduardo grin.

'She's greedy,' he said.

'Aren't we all?' was Baltasar's reply.

Soon it was all gone. The man offered her the palms of his hands in proof and she nuzzled them impatiently, lowering her head to push against him as if wheedling. He seemed to have forgotten Eduardo as he talked to the mare and teased her, love in his eyes, and she had obviously forgotten him, interested only in what Baltasar had in his pocket and at which she was now tugging with her ever eager lips.

'Ask for it,' Baltasar sharply demanded.

She responded with a shake of her head, the steel grey mane and forelock haughtily tossing as she struck the ground with an impatient hoof.

'She's showing off because you're here,' he told Eduardo without looking at him. 'Ask for it,' he ordered again.

This time she turned away as if in disgust, cantered a few strides off, returned at a trot and again pushed at his pocket, making a funny noise in her throat.

'Come on,' coaxed Baltasar, his voice all at once gentle. 'I know you're getting old but you can still do it. Show the señorito here what you can do.'

As if understanding every word, but still protesting slightly, she backed a couple of paces and went down on her knees, just as Eduardo had seen the black stallion do with Ramon, and Baltasar pulled out the carrot she had been wanting all along.

'Up you get, old girl,' he said kindly, slapping her on the neck and giving it to her.

He gave her another and then wiped his hands on his trousers in a gesture that told her there was nothing more. She looked at Eduardo for a moment, perhaps hoping he might have something to offer her, then with another shake of her head she turned away and began pulling at the poor-looking grass by the river, the bits she hadn't already eaten parched by the summer's heat.

Baltasar stood and watched her, his eyes filled with affectionate pride, and then he looked at Eduardo, expecting him to say something.

'What's her name?'

'Gaviota.'

Gull! He thought of all the gulls he had seen in Galicia, riding the waves, dominating the air currents, perching on the rooftops, attacking the incoming fishing boats in droves. 'Why's she called Gaviota?'

'Have you ever seen a gull?' demanded Baltasar.

'Plenty of times.'

'And you still need to ask that question?'

'She's a horse, not a bird. Horses can't fly.'

'Can't they? Sometimes it looks as though they are flying. If you'd seen her when she was young, with movements so pure, so free and yet so controlled, you'd have said she could fly. The Señorita Angeles always said that being on her was like flying. That's why she called her Gaviota.'

'She could have called her by any bird's name,' argued Eduardo.

'But a gull seems to hold freedom in its very soul,' insisted Baltasar, 'and that's what she gave to the señorita – freedom.'

He moved to the shade of a dark holly-oak near the river. Eduardo followed him. Gaviota went on grazing, ignoring them both, swishing her tail and shaking her mane to keep the flies at bay. There was a slight sag to her back which he hadn't noticed in his uncle's horses, but it was only apparent when she hardly moved.

'Why did my aunt come to live here?' he asked. 'If she liked horses so much she should have stayed with my Uncle Ramon.'

'If you allow me to say so, your aunt was too much like your father to be able to get on with Don Ramon.'

'But he's so nice. Everybody likes him.'

'Perhaps, perhaps.' He was obviously reluctant to say more, but Eduardo knew that servants would always talk if you pressed them hard enough.

'Tell me about my aunt,' he demanded, unbeknown to him his expression an exact image of hers whenever she had wanted anything badly.

'I'll tell you about Gaviota,' Baltasar conceded. 'Then you'll understand your aunt, too. And when I've finished,

I'll show you some things you haven't seen yet, things your father's forgotten or perhaps never knew about.'

Intrigued, Eduardo sat down under the tree and listened. Ants ran over his legs, inside his white socks and his sandals but, after a while, he forgot to brush them off.

5

Gaviota was born in the winter of 1916, near the end of January, with icy winds blowing from the sierra and not even a tree for her mother's protection. Don Eduardo preferred to have his mares stabled when their time was near, so how she came to be out on her own, a long way from the rest of the herd, was something never discovered. A negligent herdsman, or perhaps a mistake over her foaling date. However it was, she was soon missed and Angeles, who was as fearsome in her rage as her father, and who often rode this particular mare and was fond of her, took it upon herself to look for her.

She found the mare dead and the foal hardly alive. It resisted the journey to the stables across the back of a herdsman's mule, Angeles going along on foot beside it, trying to keep it alive just by her words and will-power. All the experts pronounced it would die and Don Eduardo went around shouting at everyone because of the loss of one of his best mares, but by the next morning the foal could actually stand up and Angeles had already taught it to drink from a bottle. A camp bed had been put in the stable for her but Baltasar knew she had spent the night in the straw, sharing the foal's blanket, keeping it alive with her warmth and determination.

'That foal just didn't dare to die,' he explained, 'and so she lived.'

Angeles was fifteen then, the youngest of Don Eduardo's three children, the most passionate and troublesome. When she was two, Baltasar had become her personal groom, responsible for the Shetland imported from England, because even at that age she was determined to ride and there was nothing small enough for her on the estate. By the time she was five she was racing a small Arabian mare, and although she now had two ponies Baltasar had very little to do because, right from the start, she insisted on looking after them herself.

'She could ride any horse on the estate,' Baltasar explained, 'but those that belonged to her always had her personal attention. She didn't only love riding. She also loved her horses.'

There was tremendous rivalry between Angeles and Ramon, two years her senior. Because he was a boy it was assumed he could ride better, and he always had the first choice of mounts. But for all his skill he lacked her patience, was less gentle, and never sufficiently consistent to bring out the best in any of his animals. He would tire of schooling very quickly and propose a race that might take up hours of the day. At the end of the ride he would toss the reins to a groom, but she would cool, water and feed the horse that had carried her and examine its legs and hooves for any injury.

'What about my father?' asked Eduardo at this point. 'Didn't he ride, too?'

'He had a good seat. Until he went to Madrid he rode at all the fairs, like a good son should. It was a sight to see the four of them riding through the streets of Sevilla every Holy Week, I can tell you! But he was never interested in either the horses or the bulls, much to the master's disgust. There was the Señorita Angeles racing about all day like a tomboy while he, the eldest son, preferred to sit with his books!'

It was about the time that Gaviota was born that Angeles developed a passion for the bulls which was almost as great as her love of horses. Both she and Ramon attended the annual testing of the young stock for bravery out in the pastures when, armed with a long pole, they chased after the animals on horseback and tried to knock them over. From there she went on to fighting heifers and cows on horseback in their own bull-ring.

No one ever saw her in a skirt or a dress and everyone was scandalized by her behaviour. Don Eduardo didn't know what to do with her. She was tougher and wilder than either of her brothers, perhaps because she had no mother to exert any feminine influence over her – she died only a year after Angeles' birth – and although she was tremendously self-disciplined she would accept discipline from no other quarter.

She took a fancy to Gaviota right from the beginning. Perhaps there was something feminine in her, after all, in the way she bottle-fed and molly-coddled the little filly from the very first day, giving her all the mothering she had lost. Gaviota's sire was an Arab imported from Spanish Morocco and her dam had been one of Don Eduardo's best Andalusian mares, and because she had taken charge of her and lost her heart to her, Angeles could not bear to think of the filly being turned out with the rest of the herd, to belong to no one in particular and perhaps eventually to be sold.

'She told me herself, before Gaviota was more than a fortnight old, that she was going to make her the best-trained horse in the country; that she herself was going to become a *rejoneador* – a mounted bullfighter – with Gaviota the first and best of her mounts.'

'A woman bullfighter!' Eduardo exclaimed. It sounded ridiculous as well as impossible.

She didn't tell her father of her ambitions, but when he discovered how determined she was to keep Gaviota for herself he refused to have the filly registered in her name until she promised to do two years schooling with the nuns in Sevilla. She wept and stormed about it but had to give in, though only on the condition that she could spend every weekend at home to look after Gaviota.

Baltasar took over the care of the filly in the meantime,

treating her with the same loving attention she received from her mistress. She was lively and wilful, but above all gentle. Never was a voice raised in anger against her, never was anything done to frighten her. Angeles stood at her head while she was branded, talking to her, and she hardly flinched. She was never sent out to pasture with the other mares and foals but hung around the house and stables like a pet dog, probably believing she was human, too, not recognizing any relationship with others of her kind.

When she was a two-year-old, Angeles made her a woollen headcollar. Until then she had never felt anything round her body at all, no kind of restraint. She had always followed Baltasar and the girl as she would have followed her dam, but she took to the headcollar without any problem. In all her future training Angeles never used a bit. When she was first ridden a year later, only the woollen headcollar was used and her future, intense schooling was done in a hackamore designed to exert only the gentlest of pressure, unlike Ramon's mounts, schooled in hackamores with serrated steel nosebands.

Because Ramon was always teasing his sister that one day he would ride Gaviota himself to find out if she was as good as the praises that were sung of her, Angeles decided to abandon the usual aids and have Gaviota respond to signals known only to herself. She wouldn't even let Baltasar know what these new aids were, though most of them were voiced, for she was afraid that he might one day betray her. The only time Ramon ever tried to ride her, with his sister's permission, she threw him. He mounted her three times but couldn't even get her to walk on. Each time he mounted her she behaved like a wild thing, bucking and rearing, even trying to bite his legs.

'It was the only time the señorita allowed her to be ill-used, but it was to teach her brother a lesson,' Baltasar explained.

By the time she was introduced to the bit, she responded

so implicitly to neck-reining and other aids that it was only there for adornment. Her mouth was as soft as on the day she was born – 'And remains so to his day,' Baltasar added proudly. 'She just doesn't know that metal can hurt.'

As a four-year-old Angeles could promise her brother that Gaviota had the stamina to outlast and outrun any horse on the estate, including the stallions. He immediately took up her challenge, choosing his father's best stallion with which to compete against her in a twenty-mile cross-country race. Gaviota not only got home before him but also took the ten jumps Baltasar had fixed up on Angeles' orders while they were away. The stallion refused the first jump and knocked down two others and was obviously far more exhausted than the mare.

Years went by before Angeles, in spite of every opposition, began her career as a *rejoneador*. Meanwhile she practised with her father's cows, using four different mounts of which Gaviota was always her favourite and best. For her dressage was not just an art for art's sake but the means of her horses' survival when faced with a charging bull, and even when perfection of a movement was attained she would still go on trying to find something beyond perfection.

Eventually she went to Portugal, where fighting from horseback was more popular than in Spain, and in one year alone would appear in more than fifty fights. Most of the time she rode Gaviota because she could trust her more than any other, and never once did the mare receive the tiniest scratch or bruise from a bull, even though she was so close that her flank or chest might be stained with the bull's blood. Occasionally she fought in Spain and one year went to Mexico for the season. Wherever she went Gaviota's courage and ability left the spectators breathless. She was as breathtaking to look at as to watch with her fine Arabian head and intelligent expression, and the relationship between woman and horse was by some considered supernatural. Whether

34

facing a bull or relaxing, they seemed to think together and share the same moods.

In 1930 Angeles returned home, to Ramon's home as it was by this time because Don Eduardo was dead and she had sold her portion of the estate to her brother, mostly to finance her career. There was none of the order and seriousness in the estate's affairs that there had been when her father was alive. Ramon let his head steward run most of the business, preferring to enjoy himself rather than work, and some time later Angeles, after many quarrels which were not helped by the ill-health which had forced her to retire from the ring, begged her eldest brother to allow her to move into his house.

'A year later she died of cancer,' Baltasar finished, 'and I went on looking after the mare, the same as I always used to. No one has ever ridden Gaviota but her, not even myself.'

'Why not?'

'She'd have no one else on her back. Besides, it was never my job to ride her, only to look after her. When the señorita knew she was going to die, she wanted the mare put down on the day she died. She was afraid Don Ramon would want to take her for breeding and then sell her off when she was old. He already had a black colt from her, the one you saw – Azabache. I promised I'd shoot her but it's the only promise I never kept. She seemed to know, you see, when I came out with the gun and she looked at me in such a way that I just didn't have the guts to do it. It would have been like killing a child, my child.'

'But my uncle didn't take her.'

'No. I told him that the señorita had borrowed money from your father and that the mare now belonged to him.'

'And did he believe you?'

'Your uncle believes everything they tell him. It saves him the trouble of finding out the truth.'

Eduardo didn't like this criticism of his uncle, certain, too, that Baltasar shouldn't say such things to him. But before he could think of a suitable reply, the man was reminding him, 'Tomorrow I'll take you into a room that only I have the key to. I don't think your father has ever been in there.'

He liked to tease and would say nothing more, however much Eduardo begged him. The mare had grazed right up to them by this time, sharing the shade with them. She had sniffed the boy's back and neck and left a long dribble down his bare arm which he had hastily rubbed off with a hand-kerchief. When they returned to the house, she followed Baltasar like a dog, seemingly of her own free will because all he had said to her was, 'Coming, old girl?'

'Does she always follow you about?'

'Usually.'

'Why?'

'She'd be lonely otherwise. She doesn't like to be on her own and she's got no one but me.'

'You make her sound like a person,' Eduardo accused.

'Horses like company. They're herd animals. Nothing makes a horse more miserable than being on its own. As for Gaviota, well, as you can see, she's used to a lot of affection and care. She's always had someone with her from birth. I groom her every morning and hand-feed her, too.'

'Hand-feed her?'

'Every mouthful she swallows, except for when she's graz-ing, comes from my hands,' he explained with the same pride as if he were talking about a small grandchild. 'If I must leave food in the manger or in a bucket, she won't eat it. I talk to her while she eats. She likes that and so do I. I've no one else to talk to, either.'

'You can talk to Maruja.'

'Bah! We stopped talking to each other twenty years ago, except for quarrelling. Besides, what can we have to talk about?'

At lunchtime, while Maruja was putting his plate before

him, Eduardo asked her, 'Why does Baltasar like talking to the horse more than to you?'

She answered with a snort, 'Because the horse can't answer back, that's why, and I do,' adding with a warning, 'Don't you let him start on about that horse, señorito. He'll never stop plaguing you if you do.'

Eduardo's father interrupted with a laugh. 'Baltasar and Gaviota! Which is the older of the two, eh, Maruja?'

'I don't know, Señor, but I do know that ever since Gaviota came into his life, he hasn't thought twice about me. If we'd had children it would have been different, but that mare is his child and that's all he cares about. I wish Don Ramon had taken her.'

'But then your husband would have gone, too.'

'For the difference it would have made to me, Señor, he could have taken him and good riddance,' and off she went, still mumbling bad-temperedly about her husband.

Eduardo looked at his father and they both laughed.

6

After supper that night Eduardo's father brought out two packs of well-worn playing cards and proceeded to explain the rules of Bezique. Eduardo listened earnestly but was soon lost amid the complications of trumps, tricks and scoring. His father grew impatient with him for constantly playing the wrong cards or not knowing what to do next, accusing him of being either inattentive or stupid, but then he relented and taught him something simpler as well as, to Eduardo's view, more exciting. He even managed to win a few times.

Before they went to bed his father said that the next morning he was going to see his brother again and, according to how things went, he would either be back late that same night or not until some time the following day.

'Can't I go with you?' begged Eduardo. 'I'll work while you're talking to Uncle Ramon.'

'No one works at your uncle's so you'll stay here. If I'm not back by nightfall, Maruja will sleep in the house with you.'

'I'm not scared of being on my own.'

'Nevertheless, those are my orders. I'll mark all the work I want you to do, both tomorrow and the day after, and I expect you to work exactly as if I were here. Tomorrow is the seventeenth. With a bit of luck, by the nineteenth we can start back to Madrid. You've worked quite well so far, so if you don't spoil things while I'm away you might get to

Galicia with your mother before the end of the month after all.'

'Won't you just show me how to use one of the rifles before we go back,' Eduardo pleaded hopefully. 'I've never even held a rifle.'

'They're too big for you,' he demurred. 'Still, we'll see what your work's like. If it's good enough, and if your uncle doesn't keep me too long, there might just be time to teach you a thing or two. But no touching them while I'm away, mind!'

Eduardo promised, adding eagerly, 'And will I be able to come hunting here with you one day?'

His father shrugged doubtfully. 'We'll have to see what your uncle says about that. I hope the land will belong to him after tomorrow, the house too and perhaps everything in it. That'll please your mother, no doubt. She never did like my coming here. And don't you say anything to her about hunting. That will be my affair.'

The next day, after breakfast, he was gone, all his papers packed away, his end of the big table looking quite bare and shiny. Eduardo waved good-bye to him and watched until the car had disappeared from sight before returning to the dining room from which Maruja had cleared the breakfast things, leaving only his pen and ink and school books in their usual place.

He sat down with a deep sigh, loath to begin. For a long time he stared at the big boar's head, wondering if its eyes were real or made of glass, and then his thoughts wandered on to his Uncle Ramon, his bulls and his horses. All the morning the knowledge that he was alone in the big, empty house distracted him from the long, dreary pages ticked off by his father. He played with the sunlight which streamed in through a half-open shutter; he walked round the room half a dozen times, opening empty drawers and cupboards; he watched the progress of a stray ant across the patterned floor tiles. Such was his father's personality that without his presence, inhibiting though it often was, the house was lifeless and Eduardo could think and do nothing.

By the time the two-hour study period was over all he had done was read the same page three times and drawn some pretty borders round the next two pages of his exercise book. He felt very guilty about this but just then all he wanted to do was to find Baltasar and stop being alone. He would work in the afternoon to make up for it, if it wasn't too hot for him to think.

Baltasar was waiting for him in the patio and the gleam of anticipation in his dark eyes was enough to make Eduardo forget his mood. With mounting curiosity he followed him through the neglected stables and up a narrow staircase which led to a small loft stacked with barley straw and sacks of grain. Beyond was yet another door and Baltasar pulled a giant key from his pocket to unlock it with a flourish. It opened on to a long, narrow, low-timbered attic, its gloom pierced only by threads of light from cracks in the roof until Baltasar opened a tiny window low down in the wall to let in a wide shaft of sunlight.

Eduardo immediately forgot the suffocating heat as his eyes took in the contents of that room; a wall hung with bridles and glinting bits, saddles in a line down the centre, resting on straddled racks, sheepskins and saddle blankets, javelins and banderillas and, in every available space, photographs. Some were in leather or silver frames, some were just pinned to the walls, fading and curling up, most of them showing a fair-haired, clear-eyed woman of challenging expression and undoubted beauty, and Gaviota. Gaviota in a dozen different poses – at the Holy Week processions in Sevilla, in the Mexico City bull-ring as well as in Portugal and Spain, and Eduardo could see that she had once been as beautiful as Azabache and was obviously an animal of renown.

There were posters everywhere announcing their appearance in fights, the artists hardly doing justice to Gaviota's beauty or her mistress's pride, the dates going back to before Eduardo's birth. The posters and photographs were gradually succumbing to dust and insects, but every piece of metal still shone and all the leather was smooth and supple.

'I come up here every day,' said Baltasar with pride, a jerk of his head directing the boy's attention to the pile of rags and tins of polish on a chair in one corner.

'Are they all Gaviota's things?'

'No. The Señorita Angeles had four horses, remember. You need a lot of equipment when you're travelling with so many horses. I was in charge of it all.'

'What happened to the others?'

'She sold them. Only Gaviota was her favourite.'

For a long time Eduardo wandered round the attic, watched by Baltasar whom he had forgotten in his amazement and curiosity. All this for a horse! It was beyond his comprehension. He knelt down to look out of the little window, wondering if he could see Gaviota from here.

'No, you won't see her,' said Baltasar, guessing his purpose. 'She's somewhere else today.'

Eduardo could tell by his voice and expression that he had still another surprise for him.

'Show me where she is,' he demanded, forgetting that he had ever not wanted the old man to think he was interested in her.

After closing the shutters and locking the door again, Baltasar took him to the cottage. Behind it, tied to a tree, stood Gaviota, but not as Eduardo had expected to see her, as he saw her every day.

She had a curved red plume on her head and red, white and yellow ribbons decorating her tail, almost reaching the ground. Her saddle dazzled him, its yellow and red upholstery embroidered with silver flowers, and beneath it were equally splendid red blankets, thickly embroidered with silver and gold thread, edged all round with gold tassels. Bridle, reins, breastplate and crupper – all were of dark red leather covered with a design in gold leaf. The throat latch hung beneath her chin with a gold-tasselled bell and even the long-shanked bit, curb chain and stirrups gleamed in the same metal.

She looked fit for a king or an Eastern emperor and there was an alertness in her stance, a brightness in her eyes and a palpitation in her wide-flared nostrils that made Eduardo believe for a second that Baltasar was playing a trick on him.

'She remembers, you see,' Baltasar told him. 'If I dress her up she thinks she's going to face the bulls. She liked those bulls as much as her mistress did.'

'Wasn't she scared of them?'

'Not her! She knew she could outrun and outwit them.'

'Could she still do it?'

'Well . . .' Baltasar struggled with pride and honesty. 'With the Señorita Angeles I'm sure she could, even now.'

'She's too old,' said Eduardo. 'She couldn't do anything now.'

He only said this to tease Baltasar. It seemed silly to him to have so much affection and admiration for a horse, even one that had been as clever and beautiful as Gaviota. Without these breath-taking trappings she was now only the dozy, slow-moving creature he had watched all these days. Only his crazy aunt and Baltasar turned her into something special.

7

Eduardo had lunch on his own in the dining room, but in the evening Maruja invited him to the cottage, where he watched her fry eggs and tomato over an open fire. She made it obvious that only her own food was going on to the table, wanting Eduardo to know that he was their guest. She and Baltasar quarrelled the whole time, mostly because he would keep talking about the horse of which he accused her of being jealous, and she threatened to divorce him and go and live with her sister in the village.

'Do you know,' she exclaimed, turning heatedly to Eduardo, 'it takes him two hours to walk to the village. Two hours. With that horse there, eating its head off, and he walks all the way. If that isn't crazy . . .' She rushed back to the frying pan which was spluttering noisily.

That evening Baltasar disclosed one more secret to Eduardo. He told him how he could get Gaviota to follow him anywhere, using one of the very few words Angeles had allowed him to know.

'She only ever told me the words I needed to know in order to exercise her – on a lunge rein, you understand, because no one has ever ridden Gaviota but the señorita – but I did learn a few more on my own.'

'Spying,' Maruja put in spitefully.

'Woman, one can't help overhearing things at times,' he shouted back. 'If you have her on a lead rein,' he went on, dismissing his wife with a wave of the hand, 'the only way to get her to follow is by whispering "hakma". If you don't say that, she won't move. She just digs in her hooves like a mule and you can pull as hard as you like but you won't make her move. Try it tomorrow and you'll see what I mean.'

'Not even with you?'

'Not if I don't say the right word.'

'But she follows you everywhere,' argued Eduardo, never knowing when to believe this old man or not.

'I'm talking about when she's haltered or bridled. She hardly ever is now. Today, for example, I would never have got her tied up wearing all that outfit if I hadn't been whispering "hakma, hakma". The minute you put something round her head, even if it's only a piece of string, you have to give her the right word.'

'And would she go with anybody then, even people she doesn't know?'

'If they gave her the right word.'

'Then she's silly. A thief might know it and go off with her.'

'And how could he know it? Only I could tell him. It's not a Spanish word. It's Arabic. How's any thief going to know Arabic?'

'If he were an Arabian . . .'

'Even so. He would try to tell her to come, or go, or move in Arabic and she still wouldn't move because "hakma" doesn't mean any of those things. Ah no, the señorita was too clever for that.'

'What does it mean then?'

He shrugged. 'The señorita wouldn't tell me. She said I didn't need to know so much.'

'Probably because she knew you talked too much,' put in Maruja, not to be outdone.

'Tell me some other words,' Eduardo demanded, but Baltasar shook his head.

'He's forgotten the rest or never knew them,' said Maruja with scorn.

Eduardo sat up until after midnight, finishing all the work his father had set him, wanting to gain credit as well as have the next morning free. Baltasar had promised to take him hunting with the greyhounds.

'Your father won't be back before lunch at the earliest,' he said. 'Just come and see how those dogs of mine catch us a hare for the pot tonight.'

Eduardo was longing to handle one of the hunting rifles that decorated the walls of the living room, but Baltasar said they had no need of a gun. They set off early, before the sun made walking unendurable, the two thin but well-muscled dogs racing ahead, circling, back-tracking, their keen eyes and noses alert for the faintest hint of a hare. The ground was hard, stony and hilly, covered with bushes in whose shadows grew sparse patches of faded grass.

They walked for two hours and came back with nothing, the dogs failing to set up a hare anywhere, but at least it was true about the mare as Baltasar insisted on proving. He produced a woollen headcollar and proceeded to lead her round and round the patio after gently uttering the magic word. Gaviota followed him, head stretched out, half asleep. Then he gave the rope to Eduardo.

'Come on,' he said. 'Your turn.'

The mare pricked her ears and sniffed at him as he took the rope in the way Baltasar showed him, right hand almost under her chin, left hand keeping its end from dangling. Her muzzle brushed against his arm. It was as soft as his mother's cheek.

Eduardo felt a bit silly, talking to the horse. He had never spoken to an animal before and was loath to utter a word. He tried walking forward without saying anything and immediately felt the jerk of Gaviota's head as she pulled up against him. How different she looked when her head was up and her eyes wide open!

Baltasar stood grinning at him, witholding all advice, and

there was a sparkle of anger in Eduardo's eyes as he went forward again, lips tight with determination. This time Gaviota's upward jerk pulled the rope from his hand and took the skin from his fingers with it.

'Talk to her,' said the man. 'Don't be ashamed. God didn't give her the gift of speech but he gave her an understanding of words.'

'Hakma, hakma,' said Eduardo hurriedly, cross with himself for letting Baltasar make fun of him, and the mare immediately relaxed the strain against the rope as she started to move.

'Go on,' cried Baltasar delightedly. 'Say it again. She'll follow you. Take her all round the patio at least once. But don't face her or walk in front of her! She'll not move then, whatever you say or do.'

Eduardo followed Baltasar's instructions, but only to prove that there was nothing difficult about leading a horse. He was tired of playing the old man's games. He wished his father would hurry back so that early the next morning they could be on their way to Madrid, as promised. His head ached from the heat and the two-hour walk of the morning had worn him out. He had blisters on his heels and the skin off his fingers, thanks to Baltasar.

He slept all afternoon without intending to and really expected to find his father downstairs when at last he got up. He amused himself by taking one of the rifles off the wall, in spite of his promise, and pretending to fire at the boar's head, alert for the sound of the Hispano Suiza which would give him time to put it back before his father walked in. It got boring after a while and, besides, the rifle was very heavy. Then he found the cards and tried building houses with them but tired of that, too. He kept looking at his watch, wondering why his father took so long.

Maruja came in with his supper, unable to keep from expressing her own surprise at his still being alone. She was already looking for reasons. Could the car have broken down, run out of petrol, damaged a wheel? She made it obvious that she would have trusted a mule cart through the hills sooner than the Hispano Suiza.

Baltasar followed her in, much to Eduardo's surprise. He hardly ever came into the house but he was obviously worried, too, though he disagreed with all Maruja's suggestions.

'You know what Don Ramon is. They're having a party. He won't let Don Manuel get away. You'll see,' he said to Eduardo, squeezing his shoulders. 'Tomorrow your father will come back complaining that his brother kept him far too long.'

'We're going back to Madrid tomorrow. He'll have to come back tonight.'

'What! Drive through the hills in the dark!'

'The car's got lights, woman,' Baltasar reminded his wife with a sigh of exasperation, but added, 'Even so . . .'

The two servants stayed while Eduardo had his supper, talking and sighing and saying the same things over and over again. They were all expecting his father to return from one minute to another and none of them believed any of the reasons they gave for his not doing so.

Baltasar and Maruja sat down at the table. It was getting dark and they didn't want to leave Eduardo alone. Silence fell which Baltasar eventually broke, saying, 'I ought to give the mare her feed.'

'That's all you can think about, silly old man,' snapped his wife. 'Something's happened to the master and all you can think about is that horse.'

'There you go! Scaring the boy unnecessarily. Why should something have happened? Something's held him up, that's all.'

'I can feel it. I can feel it,' she insisted, hitting her clenched hands against her chest in a dramatic manner.

'Well, I'm going to feed the mare,' returned her husband,

not wanting to give importance to her words. 'You'd better sleep here again,' he told her.

Eduardo eventually went to bed but Maruja's excited words and gestures kept him awake. He suddenly ached to be with his mother in Galicia. If he were there now she would be in the next room instead of Maruja and he could call out to her if he wanted her. Although he fought against the urge to cry, several tears slid down to the pillow before he managed to control them.

When at last he fell asleep he dreamed of Gaviota. He was trying to lead her somewhere with great urgency yet, for all that he pulled on her lead rope and cried the right word, she just refused to follow him. He was sweating with rage and anxiety, and Baltasar was standing by laughing at him while he cried out, 'Stupid, stupid horse. Hakma. Hakma.' All she did was fling up her head and refuse to move.

8

The next morning Eduardo watched Baltasar groom the mare. She was tied to the wall in the patio and stood absolutely still while the old man carefully went over every part of her body with several different brushes and cloths. He washed her eyes, her nostrils, her mouth and under her tail. He picked out her hooves, although they hardly needed attention because she wore no shoes, then he brushed them with oil both inside and out.

'To keep them from cracking,' he explained when Eduardo asked him what the oil was for.

When he had finished he untied Gaviota who immediately made towards Eduardo, ears pricked, eyes bright, odd grunting sounds issuing from her throat.

'What does she want?' he exclaimed, stepping backwards, slightly alarmed.

Baltasar laughed at him. 'She's saying hello, that's all. She seems to have taken a fancy to you. Perhaps you remind her of the señorita.'

'She couldn't remember that far back,' scoffed Eduardo, eyes expressing his disbelief.

'That's what you think. Horses have very long memories and you're the nearest likeness to the señorita she'll ever find.'

Stubbornly, Eduardo kept his hands in his pockets, resisting his urge to stroke her gleaming neck, because he knew it was what Baltasar wanted him to do. He expected everyone to be as crazy about the horse as he was.

'Come down to the river with me,' he suggested when Gaviota, after getting no attention from the boy, turned back to him. 'There's no point in hanging about here, waiting for your father to come.'

'But why hasn't he come?'

They should have been on their way back to Madrid by now but nothing was packed up or ready.

'If he hasn't returned by lunchtime, I'll go down to the village. There's a civil guard post there. They'll be able to send someone to your uncle's to make enquiries. But he'll be back before then. You'll see.'

They went to the river and Baltasar cut some alfalfa for Gaviota, who impatiently pawed the ground and shook her head until he brought it to her. There was a vegetable plot by the river, too, with tomatoes and peppers, onions and garlic, lettuces and beans. Melons were swelling promisingly among a tangle of creepers, together with zucchini and cucumbers.

'The only bit of land that's worked here,' remarked Baltasar, seeing his gaze. 'Once we had about two thousand acres under barley, as well as the olives. Most of the land beyond the river is as flat as a pancake, as you can see. Good land, too. At harvest time there'd be more than a score of reapers working from sunrise to sunset. They even slept in the fields to be sure of an early start and many of them brought their whole families along. There'd be children running about everywhere.' He sighed. 'There used to be a dozen mules in the stables. I was in charge of them all.'

'Why isn't it worked now? What happened?'

Baltasar shrugged defeatedly. 'A lot of things. It started with the tractors which your father bought to replace the mules. The villagers broke them up. Then they asked for better wages and refused to gather the harvest. There was a lot of bad feeling. The barley was all burnt as it stood in the fields. That's when your father said he wouldn't give them any more work at all. Some of the men were beaten or sent to prison. Now the government is talking of taking the land, anyway, if the owners won't work it. I expect that's why your father wants to sell out to Don Ramon.'

'How can they take it away? Why can't my father do what he likes with his own land?' challenged Eduardo indignantly.

'Because without work the people can't live.'

'Then why did they stop working before?'

'Because things were almost as bad then and they wanted them to be better.'

'But the tractors would have made things better. They make work easier.'

'With a tractor, one man can do the work of ten. And the other nine? Were they going to starve?'

Eduardo didn't know what to answer but he had a feeling that Baltasar sided with the villagers and this annoyed him. If he worked for his father he should be loyal to him, especially when he could have nothing to complain of himself. It would serve him right if, when the land was sold, Gaviota went back to his uncle.

He watched while Baltasar picked some lettuces and tomatoes and asked, 'What would you do if my father sold Gaviota with everything else?'

Baltasar stood up and looked at him.

'Don Ramon wouldn't want her now, anyway. She's too old.'

'What does he do with his old horses, then?'

'He sells them off to local people or sends them to the fair, where they go to the highest bidder.'

'Perhaps he'll do that with Gaviota,' Eduardo tormented him.

'I wouldn't give him the chance,' came the dignified reply.

'She's not your horse. You can't do as you like with her.'

Baltasar's eyes flashed. 'I had my instructions from the Señorita Angeles.'

'Would you really kill her?' he asked, driven by boredom, perversity and curiosity to plague Baltasar as far as he could.

Before he could receive any answer both were startled by a motor horn sounding a wild, exaggerated fanfaronade which not even distance could blunt. In just a few seconds – Eduardo's heart leaping with joy even while his mind doubted; the dogs at the cottage barking hysterically and then, at two sharp cracks, falling silent – both of them knew something was wrong.

Eduardo still cried excitedly, 'It's my father. He's come back,' ready to run up the hill, but Baltasar grabbed his arm.

'It's not your father,' he said, 'or, if it is, he's not alone. Those were gunshots. They must have killed the dogs.'

'Killed the dogs!'

'They're not barking any more, are they?'

Seconds passed while they stood indecisively, the car horn silent now, everything suddenly seeming more silent because of the violence of the moments before. Eduardo felt his heart racing, indignant because Baltasar held him back, frightened because he looked afraid, too.

'You'd better stay here while I see what's the matter,' the old man decided. 'No. You'd better hide somewhere.'

'Hide? What for? I want to go with you.'

'You'll do what I tell you!' Baltasar was suddenly as commanding as his father in his explosion of rage. 'Get behind those trees and bushes along the bank there. No one can see you in there if you don't move about, and don't come out till I call you. If everything's all right I'll be back in no time.'

'And if it isn't?'

Baltasar stared at him, his dark eyes as bewildered as the boy's.

'If it isn't?' he repeated. 'Well, I don't know what will happen if it isn't. But get behind those trees. Quick now. Go on with you. Do as I say.'

Eduardo was about to run off when Baltasar stopped him.

'You'd better take Gaviota with you. I don't want her getting in the way.'

'But I don't know how to – '

'Ay, how useless you are,' exploded Baltasar. 'Come, I'll take her. But let's be quick. My wife's there alone. I don't know what might be happening.'

As he spoke he pulled a piece of plaited string out of his pocket, not very long but enough to hold round Gaviota's neck. She sensed his urgency and snorted nervously, but a few words from the man calmed her. She trotted along beside him, Eduardo running ahead and looking back every few paces, urged on by Baltasar who was growing more jittery all the time. The thick holly oaks, surrounded by tall, frondy bushes, thistles and wild barley stalks made a good hiding place.

The old man wasted a few minutes making a hobble with his piece of rope.

'She hates being tied like this,' he told Eduardo, 'but the rope isn't long enough for anything else and she won't stay with you otherwise. It's a bit tight, but it won't be for long. I'll come back just as soon as I can, I promise you.'

Then he was off and Eduardo didn't know if his last words had been directed at the horse or at him. He came out from the hiding place to watch him climb the hill, stumbling in his hurry. From time to time he lost sight of him between the trees. Already Eduardo had forgotten his fear. Baltasar was just being silly, exaggerating as usual, but then he had left the mare, too, so he must be frightened of something.

Gaviota wasn't at all happy. She made funny noises in her throat, shook her head a lot and kept trying to separate her front legs, almost falling over in the attempt. Eduardo moved out of her way. He still didn't trust her too much.

In spite of the bushes the sun found him, the sun and the flies. The sun gleamed through every branch with its mid-morning intensity and shadows shrunk to a minimum. The

54

flies, originally attracted to Gaviota but tempted also by the sweat that ran down his face and neck, couldn't be kept off either. They kept buzzing round and round, some of them big horse flies that stuck to his arms and legs and stung deeply.

Several times he went down to the river to cool himself and drink the water but he didn't stay there long in case someone should see him. Besides, the water almost dried on him as he washed and the flies were very soon back again. Gaviota managed to hop down to the river, too, and stood for some time sucking up long draughts of water, her ears working back and forth. Then she struggled back to the bushes again, the only shade, heaving with effort.

For a long time Eduardo watched the hillside, until his eyes ached and he thought he could see things that weren't there. Eventually he fell asleep, letting the flies crawl where they would, unaware of the ants that marched up and down his outstretched legs and inside his sandals.

He awoke to the most dreadful hunger. All he had had that day was a bowl of Maruja's not very good coffee and a piece of bread. He could see the tomatoes in Baltasar's plot only a hundred metres away. The sun was cooler, shadows were longer, there was a breeze towards which he gratefully turned his burning face. His watch told him it was almost six.

Why hadn't Baltasar come back? Was he deliberately leaving him there to punish him for teasing him earlier? Did he only want to frighten him? But then, where was his father? If he had been in the car he would have come to look for him. He wouldn't leave him all this time.

The very silence and tranquillity were sinister and Eduardo felt panic creeping into his heart. A sudden movement of Gaviota's startled him. He had forgotten she was there. Now he was certain something was wrong. Baltasar would never leave her for so long.

In growing misery Eduardo went on waiting, playing with

55

stones, drawing pictures in the dust with broken twigs, trying to forget his hunger and fear, wondering what he should do if they never came for him at all. He could never get beyond wondering because he just didn't know what he would do.

Suddenly he heard shouts and hope flushed through him as he jumped to his feet and looked over the screen of bushes. People were coming down the hill, hurrying from what he could make out between the trunks and branches of the neglected olive trees. First he recognized Baltasar and Maruja. He was pulling her along and both of them were in full flight, only neither of them was going very fast, especially Maruja who was only kept from falling flat out by her husband's steadying arm.

Another man was coming behind them. He was doing the shouting, telling them to stop, but he wasn't hurrying as they were. He had a rifle and Eduardo saw him raise it to his shoulder and fire.

Incredulously he watched Maruja collapse at the explosion, sprawling headlong over the stoney, ochre-coloured earth, dragging Baltasar down with her. Then, as he struggled up again, trying to pull the woman up with him, there was a second echoing crack and Baltasar jumped backwards with a cry, falling a bit lower down the hill. He made an effort to get up, almost managed it, but the rifle sounded yet again and this time he crumpled without a sound.

The man with the rifle went back up the hill, and if Maruja and Baltasar hadn't still been lying there Eduardo would have thought it had all been a dream. They couldn't be dead, not just like that. Not just like that. But they were, because they didn't get up and they didn't move.

9

Nightmares usually start like ordinary dreams. Not until fear has the dreamer in its grip is there any difference between them. In the same way Eduardo's day had started until the senseless shooting of Baltasar and Maruja had turned his apprehension into outright terror, and then all that followed was a timeless, harrowing nightmare from which there was no escape.

He was too frightened to return to the house, too frightened at first to move from his hiding place, too frightened even to think. But at last he thought of his uncle's house, where he knew his father must still be, and he clung to this idea because he had nothing else to hold on to.

An hour's drive in a powerful car is two days' walking for a small boy starting out with blisters on his heels and only a few tomatoes in his pockets, grabbed in terrified haste from the plot near the river. Night fell before Eduardo had gone much beyond the first hills but the stars were so plentiful, the moon so bright, the breeze so encouraging that he was able to walk on in the darkness for quite some time. The memory of his volatile uncle and laughing cousins was very cheering and he pretended he was on a march, like the one he had done when he was at summer camp with the school only the year before. He tried to remember the words of the songs they had sung to make the marching easier, and he wasn't aware of having found somewhere to sleep until he was wakened by the glaring sun the next day.

As soon as he opened his eyes the nightmare was back, tearing at his stomach with long-nailed fingers, reminding him when he stood up of the blisters, dirty and raw, on his heels. He cried without even knowing that he cried, so badly wanting someone to put everything right as he wandered ever more slowly through the harsh, wild sierra, its stony ground far too hard for him or any other human being.

He sang spasmodically, whenever he found himself silent, not knowing he had been silent for hours. At least, he thought he was singing, but mostly he uttered broken sobs, nose blocked, throat aching, tears occasionally sliding right down to his neck, cleaning a channel through the dirt on his sun-scorched face. He stopped to rest more and more frequently, mostly because he felt quite dizzy from hunger, the rocks and bushes ahead of him seeming to dance from one side to another.

After a while he knew he could go no further. It was just impossible. All he could think of were Baltasar's tomatoes growing by the river. His uncle's house was much further away than those tomatoes and he fell asleep crying for them because they were so much more real than anything else.

The journey back was easier, mostly because it was down-hill and because he knew the way. It was dark when he returned but there were no lights in the house or in Baltasar's cottage. Perhaps the people had gone. He didn't really care any more. He would have gone to the house anyway, desperately in need of the comfort its dark, solid walls seemed to offer. He suddenly had a vision of the yellow glow of the oil lamp Maruja put on the table every night and this memory gave him courage. However, the darkness and silence inside the shuttered house when he arrived soon swamped whatever little hope he had and, without even remembering the tomatoes, he almost crawled up to his bedroom and fell asleep.

In the morning a noise in the patio woke him. He didn't know what it was but it set his heart racing with fear. For a while he lay petrified on his bed but when it came no nearer he eventually found the courage to sneak over to the window, carefully open one of the shutters slightly and look down.

It was Gaviota, looking very sorry for herself with her front legs still tied together. He had forgotten all about her till now. Tears of relief blurred his vision and, with fear overcome, hunger suddenly hit back at him again with throbbing fury. He just had to eat something, anything. He could hardly keep his eyes open, so faint did he feel, and he almost fell down the stairs.

There was a larder just off the kitchen where Maruja had put all the things they had brought from Madrid, tinned food as well as a leg of smoked ham and a big Manchego cheese. Just thinking of everything made him tremble. He had to cross the patio to reach the kitchen, burning his naked feet, and Gaviota made a funny noise in her throat when she saw him. But just then he had no time for her. All he wanted was food.

The larder door was open and there was nothing on the shelves but half a loaf of bread, hard as a rock. Everything else must have been taken by the intruders. Eduardo gratefully snatched the bread and took it to the kitchen. He filled a chipped enamel dish with water and put the bread in it to soak, impatiently testing it every few seconds until at last he could start to break bits off and eat. He found some oil in a brown jug and poured this over the bread to give it more flavour and there was a big jar of salt on the window ledge.

By the time he'd finished this mixture he felt quite sick and bloated, with a different kind of pain in his stomach but still a pain. He became aware of Gaviota standing in the kitchen doorway and realized that if only he knew how to ride she could get him away from this place. She could take him over the hills to his uncle's house or down to the village in no time. In the village there were civil guards, Baltasar had said. Why hadn't he thought of that before?

He stared at Gaviota. She looked so large and he felt so weary. Would she let him get on her back? And if he managed to mount her, how would he ride her? He thought of all the saddles and bridles in the attic above his head and dreams and reality mingled as he saw himself riding her with plumes and ribbons, only for seconds she was black instead of grey and he was someone else instead of himself.

Reality returned with heart-jumping suddenness as Gaviota gave a squeal, tossing her head and stamping both front hooves down at the same time. He supposed he should untie the string Baltasar had put round her legs but would she kick or bite him if he approached?

By the funny little noises she made as he went towards her it seemed he was doing the right thing. She stood quite still while he knelt to look at her fetlocks and he immediately saw that the string was too tight. There was blood all round it and in some places it seemed to have disappeared right under the black, blood-matted hair.

He looked in the kitchen drawers for a knife but the cutlery had been stolen along with the food. All that remained was a broken wooden knife handle and a splintered wooden spoon. Eduardo looked at Gaviota and lifted his hands in a gesture of defeat.

'You'll have to put up with it a bit longer,' he told her, for once finding nothing strange in speaking to a horse.

Her big, dark eyes watched him until he went back into the house.

Eduardo discovered that clothes, shoes, sheets and suit-cases had disappeared along with nearly everything else. He went upstairs to the attic and found that the door had been smashed open and that everything there was gone too, except the photos and posters which had been torn from the walls and taken from their frames. Baltasar's cottage had been ran-sacked, too, but at least he found some more bread there, as hard as the first piece, and a couple of smoked herrings on a plate. The chickens were gone, the finches were dead in their cages, overcome by heat and thirst; everything spoke only of desolation.

In spite of his longing for fresh tomatoes Eduardo hadn't the courage to go down to the river for them, for that would mean crossing the hillside where Baltasar and Maruja . . . No, he couldn't even bear to think about it and so he went back to the house with his piece of bread and two herrings, aching with misery.

Gaviota's eyes were on him again and she looked as dejected as he felt. He remembered the string round her fetlocks, a problem he still hadn't solved, but just then he was too dispirited to care. He went upstairs to his bed and for a long time hovered between waking and sleeping, feeling very sick and wanting his mother so badly that his whole body ached with wanting.

10

It was his favourite soup, with shrimps and chopped-up pieces of ham and big, cream-coloured pasta shells. His mother sat behind the blue-patterned tureen ladling into each plate an almost golden, steamy cascade, pausing while Pili served the first plate to his father then returned for the second which would be his. She gave him her usual smile as she dipped the ladle twice into the tureen to fill his plate to the brim, proud of his appetite, and Pili made her usual remark as she set it down in front of him, 'Ay, Señorito, you'll never manage to eat all that!' knowing full well that he would. She tucked his napkin under his chin, still treating him as if he were only four years old, and just as he was about to dip his spoon into the soup for the first delicious mouthful, he opened his eyes. Soup, table, mother and servant vanished. Only his hunger was real!

Wearily Eduardo went downstairs, remembering the smoked herrings, and although he was hungry he ate them with distaste. Gaviota stood at the kitchen door again, watching him eat, reminding him that he still hadn't untied her legs. What could he use to cut the string? He wished she would go away and not stare at him as she did. It made him feel uncomfortable.

In spite of himself he had to say something to her. It was impossible to ignore those patient, enquiring eyes. 'All right, all right. As soon as I've finished I'll find some way of getting the rope off.'

She pricked her ears and made that funny noise in her throat again as if in answer, as if she'd understood him. Of course she couldn't have, but it really seemed as though she did, and then she began tossing her head up and down, making an even stranger noise, almost a squeal.

'Don't be impatient. You've put up with it long enough so you can wait a bit longer, can't you? Just till I've finished.'

His words appeared to calm her. She stood quite still and silent, except for her ears which kept twitching back and forth. It really seemed that she had understood him.

Whether it was just the food, or whether it was having Gaviota to talk to, Eduardo felt a good deal better by the time he got up from the table. He went outside, the earth no longer burning his feet, and looked for a sharp stone, the only thing he could think of for tackling the string. Gaviota stood like a rock when at last he knelt down beside her and began to rub at the hand-made cord with the edge of the stone, finding it very laborious because there was so little space between her fetlocks. His fingers grew sticky with her blood and for a moment he thought he was going to be sick.

While he worked he felt Gaviota's hot breath on the back of his neck. She pushed her nose inside his open collar and he could feel the silky hairs of her muzzle against his skin, brushing softly, sending a tickle down his spine. His involuntary shudder caused her to pull her head away. A few seconds later, however, he could feel her muzzle against his ear and little puffs of breath as she sniffed him. It was hard to ignore her and concentrate on the work in hand. He had never noticed before what small, shapely hooves she had, nor how slender were her long legs, black to the knee. He remembered the oil Baltasar had put on those hooves. There was no trace of it now.

At last the cord snapped and one of her legs was free. Immediately Gaviota began to move impatiently and

Eduardo had too little confidence to try rubbing through the remaining piece. At least there was no more pressure on the leg, even if the rope was still there. Perhaps later he could remove it.

He looked at his dirty fingers and wondered if he ought to bathe Gaviota's dirty legs. Would she let him? You were supposed to keep cuts and grazes very clean and put iodine on them after washing them well. His mother was always very particular about that. He wondered if it was the same for horses.

He felt very pleased with himself for having freed her legs but as he returned to the kitchen to wash his hands and saw the few remains of the herrings on the table, he suddenly remembered about the house being deserted and about being alone. For a little while he had forgotten everything!

He decided to tell the civil guards what had happened. He and his father had passed through the village when they first came to the estate but they hadn't stopped and he had only a vague remembrance of rows of low, white, almost windowless houses and a road that was only a cart track. Maruja said it was a two-hour walk which wasn't very much. There he would find someone who could solve his problems and tell him where his father was. They would give him something to eat, too. He was still terribly hungry.

With these hopes uppermost, he set out almost cheerfully after washing the dirt from his face and smoothing his hair with water. He had had to put on his sandals again and had stuffed two bits of rag round his heels to keep them from rubbing. Already he had forgotten Gaviota, eager only to pour his troubles into friendly, comforting and authoritative ears, but he hadn't gone very far along the road when he found that she was following him.

He wasn't sure about this at first because she wasn't very close and she stopped frequently to nibble flowers off the thistles, but whenever he looked back she was always there.

He began to wonder if she would come as far as the village and what he would do with her if she did. She would only be a nuisance to him there.

Perhaps the civil guards would look after her or take her to his Uncle Ramon. They would surely take him to his uncle, too, and his father would be there and between them all they would make sure that those thieves or bandits, whoever they were, would be caught and punished.

But it wasn't to be like that at all. There were no civil guards at the barracks, only a crowd of men who looked like ordinary labourers but lolled about the entrance and office as if they were now in command. The Hispano Suiza was parked outside in the street and several boys dawdled round it, some sitting on the running boards, their dirty hands caressing just about every part of it as if some exotic animal had come into their midst. When Eduardo first saw the car his heart leaped with excitement for he thought his father must be with the guards, but he soon found he was wrong.

In the shuttered darkness of the small office several men eyed him with distrust. One of them asked, 'And what do you want?' in a discouraging tone and when Eduardo asked to speak to one of the guards they all hooted with laughter.

'Let's see,' said the fellow who had first addressed him, eyes mocking. 'What do you want with the civil guard?'

Eduardo explained, his words tumbling out in a confused manner, realizing even as he told his tale that these hard-faced, rough-looking villagers weren't going to help him, understanding with a growing fear that they were probably the very men who had murdered Baltasar and Maruja as well as having stolen his father's car and everything else. His voice suddenly dried up, paralysed by the panic their pitiless stares induced.

Grey eyes wide with fear, he looked from one face to another, and in the sudden silence it was as if the only sound in that hot, smoky office was that of his own frightened heart.

'You must be Don Manuel's son,' the same man said and he grunted contemptuously. 'Well, things have changed around here, señorito. We're in charge now, as you can see. Both the land and the village are ours.'

'Give him the facts,' broke in another impatiently. 'The civil guards have been shot. And the mayor. And the priest, as well as other uncooperative people like the two you've just mentioned.' Vindictively he went on, 'Your father's dead, too. Think yourself lucky that you're still alive, and get out of here quick before we decide to do something about it. Señorito,' he added, spitting out the last word with a wild hatred in his eyes.

'He's only a boy,' remonstrated one of them.

'Yes, and living off the fat of the land when my wife and son died in misery while I was in prison, put there by his father.'

'He's a señorito!' said another, Eduardo understanding by his tone that the man was offering him the biggest insult he could think of.

'Come on, get out of here before we change our minds,' shouted the second man, making as if to grab one of the rifles that stood in a corner behind him.

Eduardo staggered rather than ran outside and for several seconds he just stood in the sunny street, seeing the Hispano Suiza and its admirers as if they were part of his nightmare, his senses rocking in time with the taunting chant the boys immediately set up as they crowded round him.

'Cry-baby. Cry-baby.'

'Leave me alone,' he screamed at them, pushing through their jogging arms and hurtling down the street, not knowing where it led to, not caring, wanting only to escape the jeers and threats and pain that surrounded him.

Women in doorways stared and shouted at him, a skeleton-thin dog loped along beside him, barking and threatening to bite his legs. It left him with a yelp of surprised pain when a stone pounded into its ribs and a few seconds later Eduardo found himself sprawling over the hard ground, his flight ended.

A woman came and picked him up, smacking the dust out of his clothes even as she scolded him. His mouth was full of grit and he could feel his upper lip puffing up as he tasted blood on his teeth. The woman went on talking to him as he stared at her senselessly, unable to take anything in. She led him into a patio, sat him down beside some giant pots of geraniums, came back with a bowl of water and proceeded to wash his face and knees.

'Are you hungry?' she asked him several times before her words came through to him and he nodded violently. She brought him a piece of bread. By now there was a crowd of women and children round him and everyone asked him questions at once.

'And your mother?' someone kept asking over and over again. 'Where's your mother?' and all he could do was shake his head while the tears poured down his cheeks, clutching the piece of bread in one hand.

'Leave him alone, leave him alone. He'll be all right in a minute. Some boys were teasing him.'

Their rough friendliness was meant to comfort him but it only added to his sense of despair. If they knew who he was they wouldn't treat him like this. They would take away the bread and thrust him out into the street again. Eventually they left him alone, although two small girls with big, black eyes stood staring at him for quite some time. They wore nothing but tattered vests and were two more figures in his nightmare.

He was reluctant to return to the hostile street but afraid to remain and become the object of another round of questioning. He pushed the bread into his pocket. It wasn't a very big chunk but it was soft and smelled good. He would save it for later, for when he had left this village far behind him. But where would he go? If only Gaviota could take him to his Uncle Ramon's.

Just then, as if in answer to his next thought, he heard shouts and the squealing of a horse. He had never heard such a sound before but he knew it was a horse and something told him it was Gaviota. So much distress was in those squeals that his heart began to pound with a new agony and he ran from the patio in search of her, irresistibly drawn by her cries.

He came to a plaza in front of the church and there was Gaviota, surrounded by men and boys. She had a rope round her neck and someone was pulling on it for all his worth, half choking her, while two men behind were whacking her rump and legs with sticks, trying to make her move while keeping well out of reach of her thrashing hooves and swearing at her with every blow. Her ears were flat, her eyes held a mad glare as she plunged and kicked, resisting all their pulling and goading, and seeing her like this, all gentleness driven away by these heartless tormentors, something seemed to burst in Eduardo's head. He rushed down upon them yelling, 'Stop it. Stop it. She's mine. Mine. Leave her alone. Don't touch her.'

'Your horse, is she?' jeered the man who held the rope as all eyes turned to look at him. 'I'd like to know where you got her from.'

'She is, she's mine, and you've no right to touch her.'

The men stopped their activities and Gaviota trembled and sweated among them, rolling her eyes, taut like a wild creature caught in a trap, and there was a savage beauty in her rage and terror as she still strained against her captors, unyielding.

'We found her wandering in the plaza. She could have come from anywhere.'

'If you ask me, she's a vicious brute that somebody turned away. Probably the gypsies,' shouted one of the men with a stick. 'She no more belongs to you than to the man in the moon.'

Eduardo hadn't the courage to point out the Casares brand on her withers, which they were surely aware of. So far they didn't know who he was. If they found out they would never let him have the horse back. They had already stolen everything else.

'What are you going to do with her? Why are you hitting her so much?' he asked, not knowing how to defend her.

'We're trying to get her to the butcher's. There hasn't been any red meat in this village for many a year. But she just won't move,' said the first man.

'You want to butcher her!' cried Eduardo, aghast.

'Come on, boy. Get out of the way before she kicks you,' warned the man with the stick.

'She won't kick me. She knows me. She'll follow me like a lamb,' he desperately replied. 'I've told you. She's mine and you can't kill her.'

'Get up on her back,' challenged a third man. 'She's just tossed me twice. If she lets you stay there I'll accept your word.'

There was general assent at this but, 'On your own head be it, boy,' added one of them. 'She's a wicked brute, I tell you.'

'I've never ridden her,' Eduardo unwillingly confessed. 'I told you she'd follow me, not that I could ride her.'

'Go away with you,' came the answer. 'You're just wasting our time. Your horse and you've never ridden her!'

Eduardo knew it was no good trying to explain. Time was running out. He would have to take a chance, that or turn away and let them do as they wished with her. Suddenly he cared about Gaviota, didn't want to lose her. She was the only thing he had left.

'All right.'

He could hardly get the words out, his heart was beating so fast with fear both for himself and the mare, and his face

was so pale and drawn that one of the men took pity on him and said almost in his ear, 'Sure you want to go through with it?'

He nodded fiercely in reply, suddenly remembering that all these men were his enemies, feeling a surge of scorn for every one of them. He went up to Gaviota who was still trembling and wild-eyed, still pitched for ferocious battle, and stroked her sweat-soaked neck. He should have said something to calm her, to make her understand that he wasn't responsible for her plight, but no words would come with all these men watching and listening.

'Do you want me to hold her?' the man with the rope asked.

Eduardo shook his head, demanding, 'Give me the rope. I'm going to take her away from here.'

Someone lifted him on to her back. It felt most peculiar to be there, his legs wide apart, all that bulk and strength beneath him and nothing to cling to should she try to toss him. Her ears were flat against her head but, apart from her trembling, she was still at least.

Carefully he stroked a hand along her neck. Even in the midst of all his fear there was something grand about sitting up there, so tall. Somehow everything looked different, smaller, from the back of a horse. He was taller than all the men. He looked down on them, their brown, unshaven faces reminding him that these were Baltasar's people, the men who had gone against his father's tractors and harvests, against his very life, men of violence and hate. He didn't want to look at them any more and turned his gaze to Gaviota's ears which seemed to express her feelings more than any other part of her.

They weren't flat any more although they were still turned back.

'Well then,' demanded the man who had given him the rope, eyes and voice heavy with sarcasm, 'aren't you going to take her away from here?'

What was he to do? All he knew about Gaviota was what Baltasar had told him. He had the word 'hakma'. Would it work? Would she move forward if he gave her that word? He hardly dared kick her with his heels in case she sent him flying over her head. He trembled with the excitement of sitting there, with relief at not being tossed off, with fear and the dread of hoping.

'Hakma,' he said softly, with as firm a tone as he could muster, his voice as trembly as his hands.

One ear pricked forward. The other seemed to be waiting for a signal and stayed turned back.

'Hakma, hakma,' he repeated, urging her as much with his mind as his voice, longing for her to save both of them by taking just one step forward. 'Please, Gaviota,' he said in his head, 'Please understand.'

After a moment's hesitation she began to move and the men stepped out of the mare's way, opening the road for her through the plaza. Gaviota made up her own mind which way she was going. The road straight ahead was clear, leading directly to the barren fields beyond the village. She began to trot and Eduardo found himself bumping about all over her back, trying desperately to keep his balance, longing for her to slow down. He grabbed hold of her mane, leaning forward, hunched over her withers, and she seemed to go faster and faster.

Soon the houses were left behind. There was the open road, empty as far as the horizon ahead of them. Eduardo had just one glimpse of it before he found himself falling right over her neck, the next second feeling the ground thudding through every bone, sky and earth spinning and crashing together. By the time he had got to his feet, still breathless and aching, Gaviota was a long way ahead, tail and head high, cantering as if she had no intention of stopping.

I I

He had nowhere to go but straight ahead, no one to rely on but himself. For the first time since all the terrible things had begun to happen he understood that he wasn't dreaming, that this was no nightmare. He was awake and reality was this deserted, dusty road with the sierra ahead of him, a hostile village behind and a chunk of bread in his pocket. Gaviota had abandoned him. His father was dead.

This last was all he could think about as he made for the distant hills towards his uncle's estate. He kept remembering the Hispano Suiza parked in the village street, covered with dust and dirty fingermarks, surrounded by sprawling boys. His father had been so proud of that car with the silver stork of Lorraine on the radiator. 'The best car in Europe,' he had said when he first bought it only a year ago. He would soon have sent those ruffians about their business.

Every Sunday they would drive to El Escorial to have lunch after strolling along the tree-lined avenues and filling their lungs with the fresh sierra air, and people would stop to look at the car as it came and went, rarely having a chance to see anything so elegant, fit for a minister. He always sat at the front beside his father who, as they went along, explained about the gears and control, and his mother would beg him to drive slowly because she was always afraid if they went at more than sixty, even though it could reach a hundred and eighty kilometres an hour.

How he wished now that he had brought home a good

school report so that his father could have been proud instead of disappointed! Tears pricked in his eyes again and with an almost savage movement of his head he thrust off the urge to cry. He wasn't going to cry any more. He remembered all the times his father had accused him of babyishness, saying that his mother pampered him too much, and decided that from now on he was going to be tough and strong.

He felt a flood of bitter hatred for the villagers. They would pay. Even if for some incomprehensible reason the murderers were not brought to justice by the law, he would somehow make them pay, and there was some satisfaction, some feeling of relief as he trudged along the hard, lonely road, in vehemently swearing out loud that he would be revenged. His heart and mind were hot with rage. Oh yes, they would pay. He would have liked to hammer them with his fists, kick, scream and tear at them.

Rage gave strength and purpose to his weary body and he didn't even notice the road as he imagined to himself a dozen ways of being revenged. Destruction filled his thoughts and kept him good company.

Just before darkness fell he spied a small orchard of apricot trees. He didn't know who it belonged to; he didn't care. He scratched his arms and legs getting over the thorny branches and barbed wire that lined the walls but he filled his shirt front and pockets with the soft, pinky fruit as well as his aching stomach. Soon after this he came to a shallow river. By then it was so dark that he was afraid to go any further, as well as suddenly discovering how weary he was. He could hardly see where he was going anyway, and crept under the bridge, old enough to be Roman or Moorish, feeling safer with its stones at his back and above his head.

The sound of the water running over the stones lulled him to sleep. In the morning, something tickling his face and ear woke him up. It was Gaviota, and he sat up with amazement, brushing the sleep from his eyes. She made that gentle, whickering sound in her throat again, as if in greeting, and pawed at the ground with the leg still bound by Baltasar's tough, home-made cord. Hanging from her neck was the plaited rope the villagers had put there. She hadn't lost it but when he automatically reached out for it, she pulled back with a snort of fear or anger and whirled out of his reach.

She didn't go very far, almost immediately turning to look back at him, her tail swishing muddy flanks. There was mud all over her back and bits of her tail were matted with it, as well as with burrs that also clung to her mane.

'You look a mess,' Eduardo told her. 'What would Baltasar say?'

Her ears immediately pricked at the sound of his voice and she pawed the ground again impatiently, blowing through her nostrils and tossing her head.

'I don't know what you want. I'm not Baltasar and it's no good going on like that,' he added as she seemed to stamp ever more impatiently, 'because I don't understand you.'

He stared at her and she stared back, tail still swishing, head tossing, and for the first time Eduardo caught a glimpse of the arrogance that was in her, even if she were only a horse. She demanded something, insisted on something, as wilful as a small child.

'If you were any good, you'd take me to my Uncle Ramon's,' he said and he began to wonder if he should try to ride her again. For one moment at least he had enjoyed that hectic and desperate experience of the evening before but, as if she could divine his thoughts, the minute he got to his feet she pranced out of his reach and kept moving off sideways as he went towards her, as aware as he was of the rope round her neck.

He didn't try to catch her. The difficulties he would have to face – getting on her back, staying there, making her go the way he wanted her to – seemed too great. He would keep on walking, just as soon as he'd washed himself and had his breakfast.

The river water was icy. It helped shake off the stiffness of his night on the ground but made the scratches on his hands and arms sting again. He hadn't cleaned his teeth for ages and wondered if they would all fall out as his mother had promised him. He sucked them hard and was relieved to find that none of them moved. He would clean them when he got to Uncle Ramon's.

He clambered up the river bank, back on to the road as soon as he'd finished the apricots he had saved from the previous evening. Gaviota came very close while he ate them, whickering again, but he was too hungry to waste any on her. She had plenty to eat on the river bank. For a moment he considered trying to grab the rope again but she looked so imperious in spite of her mud that he thought better of it. She could do whatever she liked, follow him or stay, but he wasn't going to get himself kicked or bitten on her account.

Nevertheless, he had hardly started walking when he looked back to see if she was following. She wasn't and he told himself he didn't care.

It was still very early and it wasn't hard to continue his journey under the cool, pale skies, especially when so soon the ground began to grow hilly. His uncle's estate was on the other side of the hills, of that he was sure. Perhaps by nightfall he would get there and then – well, then those villagers would see! There was such a silence everywhere that Eduardo almost immediately became aware of the sound of hoofbeats just as soon as they were within hearing distance. When he looked back, aware of a slight leap in his heart, there was Gaviota, trotting along the middle of the road, dust spurting from under every hoof.

Eduardo couldn't restrain a grin but seeing that she immediately slowed to a walk as soon as she was aware of his eyes upon her, he decided to keep on going and pretend not to care. However, as the morning progressed and the sun grew higher and hotter the sound of her coming along behind him was both cheering and comforting.

When at last he could go no further and stopped in the shade of a few bushes, legs aching, stomach hollow, eyes sore from the glare of the sun, seeing black spots which only constant blinking could banish momentarily, both he and Gaviota gave up any pretence of not wanting each other's company. She came right up to him and sniffed his outstretched legs and he put out his hand to touch her muzzle. He even let her lick his sweaty palm and she dribbled all over him, leaving yellow stains on his skin.

'Oh, Gaviota,' he sighed, almost desperately, 'when are we going to arrive?'

He spent the hottest hours slumbering with his head in the shadows. She pulled and chewed at the bushes and swept off flies with her tail, stamping now and then when they crawled on her forelegs, kicking them off her belly. They buzzed about Eduardo, too, but he was too exhausted to know. When he woke up she let him rub through the remaining piece of cord round her fetlock with another stone and she let him remove the rope from her neck. They were beginning to trust each other.

12

They met the gypsies early that evening. Eduardo's progress
had been very slow, mainly because all the apricots he had
eaten were having a very bad effect on his stomach, and they
were still hardly into the hills which they must cross if ever
they were to reach the plains beyond. The gypsies travelled
with two small covered carts, a troop of seven horses and
hinnies, half a dozen scruffy, skeleton dogs, a number of
babies and toddlers and a goat. There were three men and
two women and they were travelling in the opposite direction
to Eduardo.

When he saw them he halted and they halted, too. Gaviota
raised her head, ears strained forward, quivering with
excitement. One of the gypsy horses whinnied and she
answered him, trotting across for a closer greeting. It was a
bay colt, tied to the back of one of the carts, and Gaviota's
approach caused momentary chaos as the colt struggled to
get free, one of the hinnies kicked jealously and the dogs began
barking all round. The gypsies didn't seem to mind and stood
grinning and laughing at Gaviota's curiosity and the colt's
excitement.

Eduardo didn't know what to do. He had the natural
suspicion that everyone felt towards the gypsies, systematically
branded as rogues wherever they went. And yet they didn't
seem unfriendly and he was longing for human comfort of
some kind.

'Where are you going to, boy?' one of them asked him.

'To my uncle's.'

'And who is your uncle?'

'Ramon Casares.'

The gypsy raised his eyebrows. 'You mean Don Ramon, the bull breeder?'

Eduardo nodded and the gypsy expressed his surprise with blasphemy. They were all about him now, adults and toddlers, dogs sniffing at his legs and being kicked away.

'You don't want to go to Don Ramon's,' he said after staring at him for a while, the sharp black eyes taking in all the misery and exhaustion expressed in the boy's body and clothes.

'Why not?' cried Eduardo, already suspicious, trying not to show he was afraid.

'We've just come from there. Don Ramon sometimes has a few horses for us. Honest business, you understand. But he's not there. We were told he's gone to Sevilla.'

'Who told you that?'

'The people who were there, killing the bulls, stealing everything.' He blasphemed again, adding, 'These days it's impossible for an honest man to earn a living.'

'And why are they killing the bulls, why is everything – ' He was too bewildered to go on, not even knowing what to ask.

'Don't you know we're at war, boy?' asked another of the gypsies.

'War?' Eduardo repeated the word without understanding it.

'Sure. Everybody's killing each other, everybody's gone crazy. Thank God it has nothing to do with us. A few days ago we were in Sevilla. People were being shot in the streets in a very unchristian way.'

'But who was shooting them?'

'Well, I don't know. They seemed to be shooting each other. What business is it of ours? We're horse dealers, not gun runners,' and he spat with disgust.

'That mare, is she yours?' asked the first gypsy again.

Eduardo nodded. In a moment the gypsy was beside her, grabbing an ear, dragging open her lips to look at her teeth. She half reared, squealed and pulled away from him, getting herself kicked in the hock by one of the hinnies before darting off beyond anyone's reach and halting only when she felt herself to be at a safe distance, still intrigued by the others of her kind.

'She's only fit for horse meat or bull bait,' the gypsy said to Eduardo in a derogatory tone. 'But if it will help you out of your problems I'll give you two hundred pesetas for her.'

'I don't want to sell her,' he cried angrily.

'Then what are you going to do with her? Looks to me like you can't even ride her.'

'I'll take her to Sevilla, if that's where my uncle is,' he replied with desperate bravura. The idea had only just occurred to him.

'You're going to Sevilla? All by yourself?'

'Yes,' was his fierce reply.

'Oh, well,' the gypsy shrugged, and they all began to move away, the women collecting up the toddlers who had wandered off in different directions. While this was being done the three men stood together, talking in low voices. One of them came back to Eduardo.

'If you like you could come along with us.'

'Where are you going?'

'Towards Mérida and Badajoz but, if you like, we can go to Sevilla. There's no hurry.'

'And why would you go to Sevilla if you've just been there?'

'Well, see here. If your uncle is Don Ramon and we take you to him, well, surely he'd be grateful, no? Besides, Don Ramon's always good to us. We'd like to help a nephew of his if we could.'

This made sense to Eduardo and his heart leaped at the thought of not having to travel on his own any more. The gypsy grinned at him in an encouraging way.

'But I'm not selling Gaviota,' he warned him. 'She's staying with me.'

'Whatever you wish, señorito,' agreed the gypsy. 'Now, if you'll get your mare, we'll be on our way. Are you going to ride her, or shall we tie her to one of the carts?'

'She doesn't like being tied.'

'She'll get used to it.'

'I don't know if I can catch her but she'll follow me. I know she will.'

The gypsy shrugged and went back to his companions. There was a lot of loud-voiced arguing and swearing before eventually the carts were turned round, the toddlers pushed into them, and they started back from where they had come. Eduardo was mounted on one of the hinnies, a skinny animal with every rib showing through a staring, brown hide and harness sores on various parts of its body. Gaviota kept her distance from them all above the road. Every now and then she whinnied and the colt threw up his head and sent a shrill cry back to her.

They made a detour to avoid the first village that came in sight – Ramon's village, where Eduardo had joined in the celebrations for the local saint such a short while ago.

'There's no trusting people at the moment,' the gypsy whose name was Antonio told him in explanation. 'Those people are growing fat on your uncle's bulls.'

Soon it was dark and they halted somewhere out in the country. The horses were hobbled, a fire was built, a big slab of meat was produced which must have come from the bulls, too, but Eduardo was too hungry to care. While he waited for it to cook, Antonio persuaded him to bring Gaviota close to the encampment.

'You don't want her stolen, you don't want her to disappear, do you?' he said. 'Look, give her some of this. This will make her come.'

He poured some loose grain into Eduardo's hands, then, 'Better still,' he said, 'take the tin with you. You might need more than a handful to catch that one.'

The barley corn did the trick and while Gaviota greedily took it from his palms Eduardo remembered how Baltasar had told him she was used to being hand fed every night. She made no objection when he slipped a rope round her neck. interested only in the contents of the old sardine tin which were disappearing rapidly. She munched and pawed the ground, her ears working back and forth all the time, anxious for the grain which she hadn't tasted in several days, and Eduardo led her right into the encampment without even having to touch the rope.

Antonio wanted to hobble her but when he saw the rope burns round her fetlocks he changed his mind and instead gave her a long grazing rope attached to one of the carts. She objected to this at first but the gypsies told Eduardo to ignore her and, by the time he'd filled his hungry stomach with the meat and fruit the gypsies shared with him, she had settled down to grazing and seemed to have forgotten she was tied.

Eduardo stood and watched her for a while, only just visible in the darkness beyond the camp fire, but weariness overcame him so suddenly that he soon went back to the fire around which the gypsies were gathered and, before he knew it even, had curled up on the hard ground and fallen asleep.

13

Days went by. Eduardo lost all count of time and got into a muddle whenever he tried to sort it out. It could have been a week or a fortnight since he had last seen his father. Sometimes he remembered to wind his watch, guessing by the sun what time it might be, but the hour was unimportant to the gypsies who moved when they felt like it, ate when they were hungry or when food was available, and lived each day as it came, with never any thought of the morrow.

Eduardo tired of asking first Antonio, then Paco and then Raúl when they would reach Sevilla. He even tried asking the women, who only shrugged or laughed in reply. Or if they did reply their answers were not to be trusted.

'In a few hours,' Antonio might say, rolling over to sleep for the time already mentioned. 'By sunset,' Raúl told him and had forgotten his words when that night Eduardo wanted to know why they were still in the sierra, miles from any village. 'The day after tomorrow,' Paco faithfully promised him, raising his spirits so high that he could already imagine himself clean and comfortable again and being sent on to Galicia by train, perhaps accompanied by one of his older cousins. By the end of the week he would almost certainly be with his mother. Just the thought of her brought tears to his eyes, so strongly did his longing for her sweep over him.

The two days went by with agonizing slowness. Somehow Eduardo lived through them but as they drew to a close he knew that they were still no nearer to Sevilla than before, and he couldn't help crying from rage and disappointment, especially when he knew that the gypsies didn't care, or couldn't understand his anxiety.

One of the women took all his clothes for washing, giving him in exchange what looked like a girl's blouse and a pair of black corduroy trousers far too big for him, torn in several places. Whenever he asked for his own things back, she waved her hands wildly and pretended not to understand what he was talking about. She had such a furious temper that she soon intimidated him into silence on the subject so he was stuck with the trousers, tied up with string, the polka-dot blouse and no underclothes at all. But for his pale skin and grey eyes, anyone would have taken him for a gypsy too.

Paco badgered him for hours, trying to get hold of his watch, but he had no intention of ever parting with it. His father had given him that watch on the day of his first communion, two years earlier, but even this explanation made no effect on Paco's bargaining instincts. He asked to be allowed to hold it for a minute, just to see what it felt like, but after the incident with the clothes Eduardo had grown much warier and furiously shook his head.

Antonio made friends with Gaviota surprisingly quickly, mostly with the help of the barley corn. Eduardo was cross to see how easily she could be tempted by a few handfuls of grain. He had been beginning to think she cared for him, wanted his company, but whenever she heard the special hissing sound Antonio made as he approached, her head would come up, her ears pricked, and a quiver of anticipation seemed to go right through her. She let him stroke her neck, searching eagerly for the next mouthful of corn from the rusty tin, while Eduardo watched mistrustfully.

He didn't know what to make of Antonio, who was always the kindest towards him and to whom he had recounted most of Gaviota's history as well as his own. Antonio persuaded him to ride the mare, explaining the principles of neck-reining, helping him up and walking along beside him, telling him what to do with his legs and hands. Gaviota was very uncooperative, refusing to move unless she went with a lead-rope and the word 'hakma' to make her step out. In the first flush of eagerness to ride her, Eduardo gave no second thought to letting Antonio into this secret and the gypsy kept her moving at a trot until Eduardo had found his balance and could sit to her movements, only occasionally needing to grab hold of her mane.

'She's got good breeding,' Antonio commented at the end of the first day. 'She'd throw a fine colt.' It looked as though he'd forgotten what he had said about her the day before, when he'd offered only two hundred pesetas for her.

Every day after that Eduardo rode her at the back of the column of carts and animals, which she followed unprotestingly, occasionally whickering to the colt. Antonio had made a headcollar for her and the best hours of Eduardo's day were spent on her back, where he imagined himself a horseman of the first calibre, better even than his Uncle Ramon.

Afraid that Antonio would gain too much of her confidence, provoked almost by jealousy, he tried always to be near her when they were not on the move. He would sit and watch her graze, wondering sometimes how those soft lips could rip up the tough herbage without hurt to them, marvelling at her dexterity in nipping off just the flowers of the thistles, nestled in pockets of spikey leaves.

Watching her so closely, he could not help but realize that she was no longer as sleek and clean as she had been when Baltasar groomed her every day. He mentioned this to Antonio, who quickly showed him how to improvise by rolling a few handfuls of dry stalks into a ball with which to rub her down. She seemed to like this rough grooming and Eduardo liked it even more, this close physical contact with her the nearest he could get to finding the comfort he instinctively ached for.

Sometimes he found titbits for her, or sneaked a handful of grain from the sack in one of the carts, and no longer did he find it difficult or strange to talk to her because she was the only creature he could confide in. And she listened to him, her dark eyes often closed or half closed when she wasn't grazing, her ears attentive to his voice. She would rub her head against him, almost pushing him over sometimes, or nibble at the buttons on his blouse, and he could no longer remember when he had been half afraid of her.

In the end the gypsies deceived him. He awoke one morning to find himself completely alone, with only the rubbish they had left behind to convince him that he had ever shared their company. For a second he thought they had just forgotten him, or intended to teach him a lesson for oversleeping, but immediately he knew this wasn't the case. They were so noisy, so disorganized, taking a long time to gather up their things and move on. If they had gone in such silence it was because they had planned it all along. Now he understood they had never intended to take him to Sevilla. Perhaps it wasn't even true about his uncle being there. From the very beginning Antonio had wanted Gaviota. Now she was his.

He ran to the road but of course there was no sign of them and for a while he just stood there, too stunned to think. Such betrayal was hard to believe, impossible to understand.

A hard pain swelled in his heart, too hard for any tears. He was alone again, he had lost his only companion, and he didn't even know where he was. The silent landscape offered no solution; the metallic sun seemed to mock him. As he stood there he felt as though the devil had come on to the earth and that God had abandoned it, abandoned him. It was a frightening, terrible feeling, but he had to live with it because there was nothing to persuade him that it wasn't so.

He began walking. Perhaps he could catch up with the gypsies and somehow get Gaviota back. The heat grew more and more intense as the day passed and when he reached a grove of cork trees he just had to stop, unable to endure its full afternoon blast on the empty road. There were no creatures of any kind to be seen, except ants, and dust hung in the air in a shimmering haze. The branches of the cork trees stretched wide and low, protecting him from the merciless sky, but the red, rocky earth burned.

It was dreadful to travel this lonely way without Gaviota. Only now did he realize just how much her company meant to him. He had to get her back. He fell into a doze and dreamed she was standing over him, ears pricked, tail swishing, and Baltasar was somewhere behind her, watching them both with amused approval. 'She thinks you're the Señorita Angeles,' he said. 'That's why she wants to be with you.'

The dream was so real that he woke with a start of joy but there was only the blinding sun beyond the shadows, hunger and thirst. A slight breeze rustled through the leaves above his head but disappeared almost instantly. He began walking again, blinking away the tears of despair that stung his eyes, and now and again the breeze returned to tickle his dirty face.

Hope rose when he came to tended fields beyond a forest of oaks and olive trees. He came over a hill and below was a valley with a wide, slow river and a city. In his weariness, and from that distance, the bastioned walls, the red-tiled roofs, even the river and its Roman bridge didn't seem real to his straining eyes but it was too big and solid-looking to be a mirage. By the time he actually reached the narrow, darkening streets he was in a daze of exhaustion, wandering like a sleep-walker, blundering into people who pushed him aside in suspicion.

He sat down at an empty table outside a small restaurant, after banging his shins on a chair, and suddenly a man was towering over him, a grubby white apron round his bulging middle.

'Hey, gypsy, get away from here,' the man yelled into his face, grabbing hold of his shoulders roughly and lifting him from the chair.

Eduardo saw the creases of fat round his chin, the perspiration gleaming all over him, the threatening snarl on his lips, and fainted.

14

When he woke up he didn't know where he was, except that he was in a bed with rough white sheets smelling of mothballs. He was almost in darkness and only the very feeble light filtering through a window blind gave form to the dark shapes about him, the bedposts, the wardrobe with a mirror, a big chest of drawers. It was a very small room and all the giant shadows accentuated his sense of weakness.

Where was he? This wasn't his room, or was it? Was he dreaming or had he woken up from his nightmare at last? Struggling to remember, to understand, he suddenly thought of Gaviota and the gypsies. All that had been true. Gaviota was no dream. He could even remember the smell of her, her warmth, the gentleness of her dark eyes. And if Gaviota wasn't a dream, then the rest was true, too. Tears came, hot and uncontrollable, as he recalled his mother, his father, and was gripped anew by his haunting belief that the world had gone mad.

A woman came in and found him crying. She sat on the edge of the bed and hugged him to her, crooning as if he were a baby, rocking him in her arms, almost suffocating him in her plumpness. When his tears eventually ceased she planted a loud kiss on each cheek and hugged him fiercely again, hurting him.

'I had a son just like you,' she told him, her own cheeks wet. 'But he died. It's very late but I'll bring you something to eat if you're hungry. I suppose you are.'

Eduardo nodded fiercely. She came back with a bowl of soup, thick with noodles, and an omelette and while he wolfed the food down she told him how her husband, the inn-keeper, had carried him into the kitchen, loudly blaming himself for almost frightening him to death, and that he had been lying in this bed for several hours, unaware that both of them had crept up several times to see how he was.

The food made him feel sleepy again. He had hardly finished it when his head was seeking the pillow, the woman fading into a haze of unreality. He felt her lips on his cheek before she turned out the light and then nothing more, not even dreams.

The next morning she made him have a bath in a tub in the kitchen before she would let him wear her son's clothes, which smelt of mothballs like the sheets. As he put them on, Eduardo wondered if he had slept in the dead boy's bed. There were photos of him on the sideboard of their small living room, a dark, black-eyed boy with big ears and a serious expression.

He told them about his mother in Galicia, and about Gaviota and the gypsies. He didn't want to talk about the other things. He couldn't. He just insisted that he must find Gaviota and go to Galicia. Nothing else mattered but those two things.

'We'll find your horse for you,' Cándido, the inn-keeper, promised him. 'We have stables here, you know. You've come to the right place. But first we ought to see the authorities and find out if you can be sent back to your mother. Things are very difficult these days, because of the war, but we'll do what we can.'

'You can stay here as long as you like,' his wife, Hortensia, exclaimed. 'We'll look after you till you can go home.'

Eduardo discovered that he was in Badajoz, a long, long way from Sevilla. The gypsies had certainly deceived him.

Why, Badajoz was almost in Portugal! The streets were crowded with men he took to be soldiers of some kind with their dark blue overalls, red kerchiefs round their necks and insignias on their sleeves. They lounged about in the shadows, filled the bars and cafés, and didn't seem to behave or look anything like regular soldiers.

'They're the militia,' Cándido explained. 'From Madrid.'

The commissary was crowded with people pushing, shouting, gesticulating and complaining, the guards on duty watching them with indifference, but the official who eventually took down Eduardo's particulars, after more than two hours of waiting, was hostile rather than indifferent to his request to be sent either to Sevilla, to his Uncle Ramon, or to his mother in Galicia.

'Sevilla is impossible,' he shouted at Cándido, 'as well you must know. The rebels have been in control there since the very first day. As for Galicia, that is also in rebel hands. We have no communications with either place.'

'So what can we do?' Cándido begged as placatingly as possible.

'Try the Red Cross. Meanwhile, there's the orphanage unless you want to keep him yourself. Next,' he yelled to the guard outside the door. Eduardo and the inn-keeper were dismissed.

'We'll go to the Red Cross,' Cándido promised him when they were out in the street again. 'Some time this afternoon. But now I must get back to work.'

'What about Gaviota?' asked Eduardo impatiently. Every day she was further away from him and less likely to be found. She was more real to him just now than the Red Cross, more tangible and urgent than his faraway mother.

'We'll look for her tomorrow. We'll ask the gypsies down by the river.'

'It might be too late by then. I'll look for her myself.'

'No, no,' argued the inn-keeper. 'Anything might happen.

You come home with me,' and he took him by the arm and pushed him back to the inn.

It was crowded with militia-men and both Hortensia and Cándido were rushed off their feet to serve them. Eduardo found himself alone and forgotten in the living room. He thought of the gypsies down by the river and was soon on his way there, burning with hope and anxiety.

Women were washing there, laying out their sheets on the bank, and they directed him further along, wondering what he could possibly want with the gypsies.

'They sometimes steal children and eat them,' one of them warned him. 'You go back home like a good boy.'

He came to a place where it looked as though most of the city's rubbish was tipped into the river, where starved dogs nosed in trembling fashion, a few donkeys browsed and an old woman picked over a pile of ashes. Just beyond were the gypsies, but not the ones he was looking for. They eyed him with suspicion and denied all knowledge of Antonio, Paco and Raúl.

'If I don't find them,' threatened Eduardo in desperation, 'I'm going to bring back the civil guard. They'll know how to find them. They'll look everywhere.'

The gypsies looked uneasy at this. One of them asked, 'Why do you want them?'

'They've stolen my horse.'

'Go away with you. You never had a horse.'

'Why doesn't your father come? Children don't come here looking for stolen horses,' insisted another.

'The guards will come,' Eduardo promised them, eyes flashing contemptuously. He wasn't scared of gypsies any more.

After a long silence and an exchange of looks one of them said, 'A family did pass this way with some horses to sell. But they didn't stop.'

'Was there a dapple grey mare among them with black legs?'

'There might have been,' the spokesman admitted cautiously. 'Anyway, they sold them all and went on.'

'Sold them! Who to?'

'The municipal slaughterhouse most probably, if they managed to sell them so quickly. But it's none of our business. It's nothing to do with us. We don't even know if they're the people you're looking for.'

Eduardo barely heard his protestations, struck to the heart by the nonchalant reply to his question. Was this how Gaviota was to end her life, betrayed by a gypsy with a handful of barley corn, betrayed by himself for having given Antonio the word that would make her obedient to him.

They told him how to get to the slaughterhouse and he ran all the way, even though the sun was at its harshest, the sweat that half-blinded him and made his shirt stick to his body as much due to his fear for Gaviota as the heat. He could smell the place before he reached it – a hot, sticky smell which clung to the atmosphere and was hard to breathe in. There seemed to be neither windows nor doors, as if what went on inside the long, low building was secret or shameful. How should he get in? Who should he talk to?

Eventually he found an entrance, with a man just inside who took him along a passage and into an office where a bald man with rolled-up shirt sleeves looked over some papers. Eduardo explained why he was there, his words tumbling over each other, his throat half choked with fear and the smell that seeped everywhere. When he had finished all the man said was, 'And have you any proof of ownership?'

'She has a "C" for Casares branded on her back, that's my name,' he offered hopefully.

'For Casares, Córdoba, Cádiz and Canada,' came the derisive reply.

'But she knows me. She'd come to me if you'd let me see her.'

The man sighed, unaffected by Eduardo's urgency, directing him a look of blank disinterest.

'Without proof of ownership, if she is here the only way we can let you have her is by selling her to you. You must realize we can't give away horses to every Tom, Dick or Harry who comes asking for them.'

'But she's mine, I tell you.'

'Let's find out first if we have her.' He pressed a button on his desk and another man came in. 'See if we have a mare of this description down in the yards.' He handed him a paper he'd just written on. 'Brought in by some gypsies. Yesterday probably. Would she still be here?'

'Most of yesterday's stuff went out this morning, but . . .' He shrugged. 'There's always a possibility.'

After what seemed an age the man came back. 'She's in the last batch for this morning,' he said.

'Tell them to wait, then,' and when they were alone again, the bald man said to Eduardo, 'Well, do you want her?'

'Of course I do.'

'Have you got any money?'

Eduardo shook his head.

'Then . . .'

'She's mine. You can't kill her – '

'She won't feel a thing.'

'Please wait. I'll find the money somehow. How much do you want? The gypsies said two hundred.'

'Two hundred!' The man laughed scornfully. 'Six hundred's more likely the price.'

'I'll get it,' Eduardo exclaimed. 'It may take me a little time but I'll get it, I promise you.'

'We've no facilities for keeping her here while you find the money. I'm sorry, boy. It's too late.'

'But you can't,' he cried. 'I would get the money. . . .'

His voice tailed away. He could tell from the man's expression that it was useless to argue. Gaviota was only meat to him. She wasn't a living creature with a soft muzzle and quivering ears. His lips trembled as he turned to go.

'How about that watch?' the man said as he opened the door.

Eduardo looked back, not understanding.

'The watch. Let's have a look at it. It must be worth all of six hundred pesetas. I don't know how a boy of your age can have such a valuable thing.'

'My father gave it to me at my first communion. I can't let you have it.'

'Pity.' It was all he said.

Eduardo walked back along the corridor, anxious now to get outside and not let anyone see the tears he could no longer withold. He had said he wouldn't cry again, that he would be strong, but with Gaviota so near, perhaps only separated from him by these walls, waiting to die that very morning, it was hard to be strong. Would she be wondering why she was there? How would they kill her? Would she know she was going to die and be afraid? Suppose she refused to move out of the yard or pen or wherever she was, would they beat her?

He stopped. The man at the street door stood impatiently waiting for him. Eduardo looked down at the watch on his wrist. Even now he could remember that morning, two years ago in May, as if it were yesterday; his mother smothering him with kisses, exclaiming at his handsomeness in the dark blue sailor suit with the gold braid and buttons; his father handing him the long white box with the watch inside on a red velvet cushion.

'It's a proud day for me, my son,' he had said. 'I want you to wear this watch always in remembrance of it.'

Desperately he pulled the watch off his wrist and ran back to the office with it.

'Here you are,' he cried, thrusting it under the man's nose. 'Now let me have my horse.'

15

Gaviota was lame. No wonder Antonio had abandoned her. She was so lame she could hardly walk, hesitating before every stride, twice almost falling in the steep, cobbled lanes. Her ears were flat, her fine, beautiful head looked suddenly thin with pain, the hollows above her eyes twice as deep. In fact, had it not been for the brand on her withers Eduardo might even have doubted she was the same animal, except that she pricked her ears as soon as she saw him and made that funny grunting noise which he had come to recognize as a greeting.

It took him a long time to get her back to Cándido's restaurant and he ached with her every plunging stride, hesitating to urge her on when she halted for long minutes, head low, the injured foreleg off the ground. People in the streets gave him advice or asked him what he was doing with her. Someone looked at the leg, running his hands up and down the bone in a professional manner.

'Nothing broken, anyway,' he said. 'Could be a kick from another horse. Looks like she should have been shod long ago, too. Maybe she's just bruised the heel.'

'She'll be all right, won't she?' Eduardo begged him.

'I expect so. Plenty of bathing and rest should put her right. But get her shod before working her again.'

His hopeful words lifted a load from Eduardo's heart and even Gaviota seemed to sense his sudden cheerfulness, making an extra effort so that they got half way down a street without stopping. Cándido and Hortensia made a lot of fuss when at last he arrived, scolding him for running off, scolding even more when they discovered he had exchanged his valuable watch for a lame horse.

'You can't be sure she'll get better,' Cándido told him. 'It was a foolish thing to do. Besides, if you do get sent to Galicia you won't be able to take the mare with you. There's no room for horses in trains just now.'

Eduardo hadn't thought of that but just then he was too weary to care. The emotions of the day had left him drained. In fact, he looked as haggard as the mare and Cándido took pity on him at last, giving him a few coins to buy straw and barley corn after getting her into the stable.

The stable was wide and dark, its only window covered with cobwebs and cluttered with old tins. There was a long stone manger into which iron rings were embedded for the tying of up to a dozen animals. The floor was soft with the droppings of years as well as all the kitchen waste that Hortensia threw down there and the loft above was used by drovers or muleteers when they stayed the night.

Eduardo tied Gaviota at the far end, where she wouldn't be troubled by visiting animals. He tipped her feed into the manger but she snorted and pushed her nose against his chest until he realized that she was waiting for him to give it to her himself. Then she ate greedily, as if it had been a long time since she had filled her belly, and a lot of the chaff and corn fell on to the floor because Eduardo's hands were small compared with Baltasar's and she was so anxious. It took him a long time to feed her like this but he didn't care, smiling to himself as he watched her munching jaws and flicking ears, forgetting everything in the pleasure of the moment.

Hortensia brought him a bucket into which he persuaded Gaviota to lower her injured leg. At first she was very much against his intentions but when he started splashing the water over it, she seemed to sense it would do her good and let it down. There was so much heat in the swollen fetlock that even in the water Eduardo could feel it. He knelt beside her and talked to her while his hands stroked up and down the bone and round the hoof, and he no longer remembered ever being afraid of her or caring about her dirtying his clothes or hands.

Several times a day Eduardo bathed her leg until a week later all the swelling and heat had gone and she stood as firmly as before. She snorted with pleasure whenever he came to her and he could hear her whinnying plaintively whenever he left her alone. He tried not to leave her alone too much, knowing how much she liked company, and he made a wisp with some straw from the feed merchant's with which to groom her while he talked to her, smoothing her fine skin with old rags from Hortensia's kitchen.

He rescued a big round sardine tin from the dustbin and held this in one hand while he fed her with the other, so that none of the bits were wasted on the floor. Cándido grumbled every time he handed out cash for her feed and wasn't over generous with it. Eduardo knew Gaviota was hungry as well as impatient, tied in the stable, but there was no grazing in the city, except on the river bank, and he was afraid to take her down there. He didn't dare ask for the money to have her shod.

He would have spent most of the day with Gaviota except that Cándido expected him to help in the restaurant in exchange for keeping Gaviota as well as himself. With so many militia-men in the city the tables were nearly always crowded, so Eduardo learned to collect dirty plates and glasses, clean tables, sweep the floor, refill the wine glasses and run all the errands. He hated the work, mostly because he was afraid of all these blue-overalled men with their talk of war and death, and also because he felt such an occupation was beneath him. The customers called him 'boy', expecting him to come running when they clapped their hands, and they often teased him or played tricks on him.

He wrote to his mother, begging her to come for him as soon as possible, sure that she could find a way. He began to tell her about his father but stopped, unable to put down on paper what had happened, getting no further than the word 'Papa'. After wrestling with himself for an endless time, fighting in his head with things he didn't want to remember, he rubbed even that word out, so hard that he made a hole in the paper. Instead he put, 'Aunt Angeles' horse is with me. I hope she can come to Galicia, too.'

Hortensia posted it for him the next morning, as ignorant as he was of its possible fate, and from then on Eduardo counted the days, sure that a reply must come before the week was out. Gaviota fretted in the stable, lacking exercise, but Cándido was against Eduardo taking her out by himself.

Refugees were beginning to converge upon the city, bringing tales of death and destruction along with whatever few things they had salvaged from their abandoned homes: mattresses, pots and pans, suitcases, sometimes a canary in a cage. Most of them were making for Portugal and their transport was often no more than an overloaded cart pulled by an overstrained donkey.

'They'll steal Gaviota if they can,' Cándido warned. 'Some of these people are as bad as the gypsies.'

Their faces reminded Eduardo of the people of his father's village and he was glad to have Gaviota hidden away in the dark stable. Everyone said that the enemy was coming, that the city would be attacked soon, and sometimes Eduardo wondered who the enemy was. For him, the enemy were those who had killed his father, Baltasar and Maruja, and who had driven his uncle away. Were they coming? He asked Cándido one day if he knew who the enemy was, terrified by the very thought of an army of villagers, even though the men in blue were there to defend the city.

'It's the Army of Africa,' Cándido told him. 'They're the ones who started it all. But they won't take Badajoz, even though they've got Sevilla. There they had no opposition but here. . . . Here, things will be different. In this city we'll die before we surrender.' His eyes blazed and his face grew hard with determination as he spoke, giving him an unusually impressive appearance.

Eduardo escaped to the stable, needing to think.

The Army of Africa! The Legionnaires! The élite of the Spanish army, so his mother had once told him. Her younger brother, his Uncle Teodoro, was a lieutenant in the Army of Africa. If he was coming then everything would be all right. He would see that he got to his mother. He might even find transport for Gaviota. He remembered his uncle, a tall, blond man with two stars on the sleeve of his uniform and a tassle on the front of his cap.

In his first enthusiasm he forgot that Cándido had called him 'the enemy', but now he remembered and was confused. His fear came back, shades of his nightmare world where friends were enemies and enemies were friends. If he told Cándido about his uncle, what would he do? Hand him over to the militia? Send him to the orphanage? Would Hortensia stop caring for him and calling him 'son'? Both were as kind to him as ever Baltasar and Maruja had been so they couldn't be bad. They wanted him to get home to his mother and yet if his Uncle Teodoro were to come now Cándido might try to kill him.

In his confusion and distress Gaviota was his only consolation. He fed her and talked to her and made her hide gleam with his straw and rags, longing for things to be as they always had been. She at least was his certain friend.

16

The Army of Africa attacked Badajoz on the fourteenth of August. First of all they took Mérida, only a day's journey away, and a few days later, like a machine that couldn't be stopped, rolled on to the trembling, waiting Badajoz, singing their battle hymn, 'Long Live Death'.

The first Eduardo knew about the attack was when artillery shells began exploding against the walls of the houses and shops, the guns he had heard only as a rumble before now almost deafening him from the other side of the river. Stone, plaster, bricks flew in every direction, together with the splintered shells which stopped in the bodies of anyone who happened to get in their way. People ran about everywhere, dashing out of stricken buildings, searching for safety, or just not knowing where they were going, and soon the human agony of warfare was added to the noise of cannon and shell.

Gaviota whinnied with fear in the stable, her eyes rolling as she pulled against the rope that held her, and Eduardo, who was just as frightened, didn't know whether it was safer to stay there in the half dark and hope that the house wouldn't fall down on top of them or to take her out and run for it, which seemed to be the idea of most of the neighbours.

Cándido had pulled off his apron, put up his shutters and closed his doors, shouting that he was off to fight at the walls if only he could find someone who would give him a gun. Hortensia was in hysterics, begging him to stay, reminding him he was too old for such things, but he went anyway because someone came to tell him that the civil guard was in revolt and had to be quelled before they could turn their full force on the enemy beyond the river.

Eduardo stayed in the stable, trying to keep Gaviota calm, and he bit his tongue talking to her, jittery with fear. Every single word had to be forced out because his mouth and throat wouldn't work properly, and in the end he gave up trying to talk, clinging to her neck instead and getting his nose bruised and his foot trodden on. Hortensia tried to drag him away, saying it would be safer in the church, but he couldn't take Gaviota to the church and he wasn't leaving her alone. She insisted, then pleaded and cried, but she went away on her own.

Eventually Eduardo crouched down in a corner, between the manger and the wall, shuddering with every explosion, just like Gaviota did, watching her but unable to console her except by not leaving her to struggle with fear all alone.

Some time after midday the shelling stopped. The silence that followed was more terrifying than the noise. What was going to happen now? Eduardo made a dream for himself

of his Uncle Teodoro coming, flinging open the stable door, pulling him into his arms and swinging him round in a bear-hug with a yell of delight. But it was only a dream because Uncle Teodoro never came.

The noise started up again some time later – he had no idea exactly when – only this time it was machine-gun fire and explosions, coming from various directions. In the street outside there was mostly silence. Every now and then a tremble ran right through Gaviota's body but she was calmer than before and looking for something to eat. Eduardo had no money to buy her food. Besides, the feed merchant's would surely be shut. He went to the kitchen and found some carrots and fruit, as well as the bread for that day, and he shared this with her, not caring what Cándido and his wife might say when they returned.

Hortensia came back soon afterwards to tell him that all the militia and a good many of the ordinary citizens were crowded at the entrances to the city and its walls, trying to keep the army out. Very soon wounded men were dragging themselves or others back into the centre. Many of them, dazed and blood-stained, came and sat at the tables outside on the pavement, some of them calling out for assistance, others just slumping down on the ground without a sound. Eduardo watched, horrified. Only yesterday men like these had been banging on the tables to make him run faster to serve them.

Hortensia yelled to him to fetch sheets which could be torn into bandages but her strident voice was all part of the horror and he couldn't take it in. He ran back to the stable, to Gaviota's safe warmth and friendly whickerings. He didn't want to know about the world outside.

But he couldn't escape it altogether. The walls were breached and the fighting went on in the streets all over the city. Eduardo could hear it just beyond the stable wall: shots, running feet, screams, shouts. Even when night came and

Gaviota was only a dark shape and a warm smell somewhere near him, the fighting went on. Now and again she grunted hungrily, pawing the ground, shaking her head, extremely restless, her hind quarters moving from side to side almost trampling Eduardo in his corner at times. The night and the fighting went on and on.

The stable door suddenly opened and Cándido stood there, gently calling his name. He was holding an oil lamp and his face looked yellow in its glow, much older, thinner.

'You can't stay here all night,' he said.

'Gaviota's hungry.'

'Tomorrow we'll find her something to eat. My wife's made some soup. Come and have some. Then go to bed.'

'I'm sick,' said Eduardo dully. 'I don't want to eat.'

It was true. His whole body felt battered and churned up. He would rather have stayed in the dark with Gaviota.

There were several wounded militia-men and others in the kitchen, drinking Hortensia's soup, with harassed expressions of nightmare quality, too silent to be natural, and in the restaurant beyond there were men asleep on the floor. Hortensia took him up to bed, helped him off with his clothes and pulled the sheet up over him because he was too uncaring to do any of these things for himself.

She gave him a kiss and said, 'Things will be better tomorrow. You'll see.'

'Gaviota's hungry,' he mumbled.

'You can buy her some barley tomorrow, double quantity to make up for today.'

'Can I really? Is everything all right now?' but he didn't hear her answer, too quickly asleep.

In the morning shouts and a battering on the restaurant door woke him up. He was too scared to go downstairs but he peeped beneath the window blind and saw all the men who had been in the kitchen and restaurant the night before being flung into a group of Moorish soldiers who waited in the street with bayonetted rifles at the ready. Cándido and Hortensia were among them, clinging to each other with bewildered, frightened expressions. Neighbours stood by in silence.

Suddenly the bedroom door burst open and Eduardo found himself face to face with a couple of Moors who, knives in hand, proceeded to pull the mattress off the bed, drag out the contents of the wardrobe and chest of drawers and look under the bed itself before going on to search the rest of the rooms in the same way. They spoke not a word to him, but their few seconds' destruction put him into a state bordering on collapse, such was the impression given by the first murderous, black-eyed stare directed at him. A long time passed after they had left the house and the street, herding off their captives, before Eduardo's heart began to beat normally again but nothing could rid him of his dreadful fear.

He waited half the morning for Cándido and Hortensia to come back, dividing his time between the stable and the kitchen, shaking every time there was a burst of machine-gun fire or rifle shots somewhere in the city. He remembered when he had waited with Gaviota before, when Baltasar had promised to return for him. The running through the trees, the shots, Maruja falling and then Baltasar – it all flashed back to him in an instant of horror. This dread-filled waiting was the same. Everything was being repeated. Fearsome memories engulfed him in a wave of sickness.

But he had to think of Gaviota. She was hungry, dreadfully hungry. He ventured into the street, hoping to get some barley for her, but the feed merchant's shop was still shuttered. Someone said he was dead, and he had been such a friendly man.

Back in Hortensia's kitchen, Eduardo filled a wine-skin with water and a chequered napkin with some pieces of sausage and a strip of dried cod, all he could find that was immediately edible, determined to take Gaviota away, out into the country where there would be grazing for her and no overwhelming sense of fear and destruction such as hovered in the very air of the city that day.

He had forgotten that he had wanted the Army of Africa to come. Blood and death were all around him and he wanted to run away. Perhaps everyone was bad now and only the ones who died were good.

17

In the fields beyond the city the corn had been cut but the stubble remained and Gaviota grazed her fill of it, dappled skin gleaming in the sunlight. Eduardo had taken her a good way off the road, fearful that she might be stolen from him by some of the desperate people running away from the defeated city. He had found an olive tree in whose shade he lingered while Gaviota ripped up the dry, crackling stalks only a short way off. She had satisfied the worst of her hunger, and now and again stopped to look up at him as if to assure herself that she wasn't alone. She was beautiful when she gazed at him in this way, not with Azabache's wild masculine beauty but with an air of proud-heartedness and affection.

In this vast, unending meadow, its ochre yellow broken by the shadow of grey olive trees, Eduardo could forget all that he had been through in the last twenty-four hours. There was a tremendous silence, disturbed only by the stubble cracking under Gaviota's hooves and the occasional cry of a quail; and a tremendous peace which he so desperately needed. Gaviota came to stand under the tree with him, head low, eyes closing, and the sun blazed over the stubble beyond until it became an incandescent lake. If only they could stay here forever, protected by the tree's shadow, surrounded by silence. . . .

As evening approached Eduardo decided that they ought to start walking. If they walked in the evening and rested during the day, giving Gaviota plenty of time to graze, travelling wouldn't be so hard and perhaps they could get to Galicia on their own. He made calculations in his head, trying to remember the geography he had been obliged to learn parrot-fashion at school. The province of Badajoz was followed to the north by that of Cáceres. Then came Salamanca and Zamora. He got stuck there for a long time, unable to recall what followed Zamora to the west, but having something to think about made him forget all the walking he had to do.

Gaviota went along beside him, not needing the rope round her head, not noticing that he held it. There was no one on the road now and so he had taken to it again, afraid of losing himself in the meadows which stretched into the distance, seemingly into nowhere. He didn't know where the road would take him but at least it was going northwards which was where Galicia lay.

Of course, if he could ride Gaviota they would reach home in next to no time but how was he to get on her back? She was far too tall and he was far too inexperienced to be able to spring up there. Also she took very unkindly to his clumsy efforts at pulling himself up, refusing to stand still, circling away from him, even rearing slightly with little squeals of annoyance.

'Oh, Gaviota, if only you'd let me ride you, we'd be home so soon!'

His voice made her snort appreciatively and rub her nose against his shoulder but, of course, she didn't understand what he said.

Home! In many ways Galicia was more like home than Madrid because that was where he enjoyed himself most. In Madrid it was all school and homework, with his father rarely at home and too busy to talk to him when he was, and his mother's time taken up by her many friends with whom she discussed dull things like fashion and hairstyles or played cards. In Galicia his parents were different people, relaxed by the holiday atmosphere. Quite a lot of people went to the town for their holidays because of its good beaches and cool climate. That was how his father had met his mother there, while on holiday with some friends from Madrid. They had met at a dance and after that, for the next five years, his father had returned every year to dance with her again, writing letters between times.

'Most of our courting was done by post,' his mother had once told him, showing him the pile of letters she still kept, but not letting him read any.

Perhaps they would stay in Galicia now because they had no relations in Madrid, only it wouldn't be the same any more. He would have to look after his mother now; make sure that she rested; accompany her to the doctor's; keep her from worrying about things.

Thinking like this, his determination to return to her as soon as possible made the road less wearying. The horizon was growing darker, the sun was fading when, a little way ahead, he made out the shapes of a big, two-wheeled farm cart parked on the roadside with people in it and several men walking round it. The cart was resting on its shafts and there was no mule, horse or donkey anywhere near as far as he could see. The men were dressed in blue and, with a start, Eduardo realized that they were militia-men.

He stopped, wondering if he had time to escape into the fields with Gaviota, wanting nothing to do with soldiers, too vividly remembering them bleeding and dying at the restaurant tables. But they were far too close and very purposeful in their stride.

'Hey, boy,' one of them called. 'Bring us that horse. We need it.'

Instinctively he clung to the rope with both hands. Gaviota snorted, sensing his sudden distress, taking a few steps backwards. Then the man had his hand on the rope, too, and he looked at Eduardo with hard eyes, his unshaven face haggard with fatigue.

'Come on,' he said. 'We need her. Don't waste time.'

'Why do you want her? She's mine. You can't have her.'

'See that cart back there?' He jerked his head towards it. 'It's loaded with wounded men. They can't walk. My mates and I have been pulling that cart all day, for want of a beast of some kind, and we can't go any further. If the Moors catch us they'll murder every last one of us, so we're taking your horse – requisitioning it, if you like.'

'You can't have her,' he insisted, dumbfounded, knowing that they were going to take her anyway. 'She can't pull a cart. She doesn't know how to.'

'She'll learn,' said another, 'once she's hitched to it. Come on, don't let's waste any more time.'

Gaviota reared up with a squeal as this second man pulled the rope from Eduardo's hands and dragged on it.

'No games with me, fine lady,' he said threateningly. 'Come on, boy, you take her to the cart. She knows you. She won't make trouble like that and we'll save time.'

'I won't,' he cried. 'I need her as much as you do. She's going to take me to Galicia.'

'Look, you can have her back just as soon as we catch up with one of our divisions or find somewhere safe to leave our injured. You wouldn't want those Moors to slaughter us, would you? They'll be coming this way pretty soon, I shouldn't wonder.'

'Either you help us or we'll manage without you,' the first man said. 'Cut the talk and get moving.'

There was no refusing them and in no time at all the harness was out of the cart and fastened round her. It didn't fit well, obviously meant for a mule a lot fatter than she was. She snorted and trembled when the collar was pushed over her head and wouldn't back between the shafts of the cart. Eduardo didn't know how to make her but with a man on either side of her, pushing on her shoulders and putting all their weight against the sharp metal noseband, they soon got her where they wanted her. Her heavy, strangled breathing frightened Eduardo.

'Don't hurt her,' he begged. 'She doesn't know what you want.'

'We've no time for delicacies,' was the rough reply and they tried chaining her up with many an oath because she wouldn't keep still until the fellow who obviously knew about horses twisted the rope tightly round her nostrils, squeezing that soft, sensitive part of her in such a vicelike grip that all she could do was roll her eyes, give shuddering gasps and stand still.

Eduardo could do nothing to help her. The whole scene was another of those nightmare happenings, too real to believe; barbarous fantasy with the ghastly faces of the helpless men in the cart too dreadful to be looked at, yet he a terrified onlooker, sharing their mute suffering.

They pulled him on to the cart, disregarding his warnings that Gaviota wouldn't go for them, turning deaf ears to his pleas, and she went for them, even though she had never drawn a cart before and in spite of its weight. The noise of its wheels, the shouts of the men and the slapping of the reins across her rump made her set off at breakneck speed, such as Eduardo could never have imagined. She fled from the cart, from the men, from her fear, bolting blindly along the road with ears back, neck stretched out, the picture of a thing gone mad with terror, and the driver encouraged her with loud yells, heedless of his passengers who were jolted into each other and cried out in protest and pain.

In spite of her fright, Gaviota couldn't keep up such a pace for very long. The cart was far too heavy, the road far too hard for her unshod hooves. She halted of her own accord, paying no heed when the driver slapped the reins and yelled at her, flanks heaving, head drooping, and this time it took

Eduardo to get her moving, walking at her head and encouraging her with the word 'hakma'. The driver had been all for putting the twitch on her again and dragging her forward like that but to Eduardo's relief she obeyed his signal, though it cut him to the heart to see how she laboured, honestly if unwillingly. She couldn't even see him because of the blinkers but she responded to his voice, trusting him.

18

All through the night Gaviota was kept on the move. Once she understood what was required of her and no longer fought against the cart and its driver, she plodded at a steady pace, a machine now rather than a living creature. Eduardo didn't remember getting back into the cart and falling asleep somewhere among the legs and bodies and rifles of the wounded men. He awoke, as they did, to the rough jerking as the cart was pulled off the road early the next morning to give Gaviota a chance to graze and the driver to sleep.

The man refused to take off her harness, in case they needed to depart in a hurry. It took the three healthy men long enough just to get their wounded comrades out of the cart and lay them down in the shade. Eduardo turned his head away and tried to shut their groans and curses from his ears. It was still cool, the sun was hardly up, and he stood beside the mare unable to think of anything to say to her, to affected both by her misery and the men's.

'Please let us go now,' he begged the driver when he was stretched on his side beneath some bushes, a rifle beside him on which his hand rested. 'She can't go any further. She's even too tired to eat.'

This was true. The grass was there, not good green stuff like in the fields of Galicia, but the kind she was used to, and yet she didn't want it. She sniffed over it, blew through her nostrils with hanging head, but didn't eat.

'She probably wants watering. See if you can find some

water round here instead of whining, and let me sleep. We've got two hours, that's all, before going on again.'

There wasn't any water, only a dried-up stream bed which probably hadn't run with water since winter. There was nothing left in his wine-skin, the men had none either, or any food, and the land was like a desert, offering nothing but hard ground, dust and despair.

They went on again through all the heat of the morning, leaving one young fellow behind, the men in the cart mostly silent, the driver only opening his mouth to urge on Gaviota when she seemed to tarry; fantasy figures which the sun might have created in one of its many mirages. The cart creaked, Gaviota's hooves made a muted rhythm, going slower and slower all the time. Eduardo walked much of the way beside her, trying to keep up both his spirits and hers with his voice. But it was too hot to talk, too hot to think or even feel.

Again they rested and again they went on, Gaviota stumbling frequently, her hooves split by the hard road. She was so jaded that Eduardo cried for her, sure she would drop down dead if they didn't have mercy on her soon. The heavy, ill-fitting harness had rubbed sores into her tender skin, which was soaked with sweat in spite of the heat that dried up everything, and Eduardo longed for her to give in, to prove to these men that she could do no more. What made her keep on he just couldn't understand. Was she stupid? Did she do it because she believed it was what ne wanted? He put his arms round her neck and sobbed into it. She was letting them kill her and he didn't know why.

Somewhere along the way she stumbled again and fell on her knees. Eduardo heard the shaft crack as she rolled on to it and the driver uttered a loud oath as he jumped down from the tottering cart.

'We've had it now!' he exclaimed and swore again.

Gaviota wouldn't get up, not even when the harness was

removed after a tremendous struggle. She just lay across the cart shaft, eyes empty, corpse-like except that every now and then she shuddered and kicked compulsively.

'You've killed her,' Eduardo cried at the men who stood round her staring, hating them, hating them so much.

'Sorry, boy,' one of them said. 'You know how it is. The war . . .'

'She's got nothing to do with wars. It's not her fault.'

He knelt down beside her, feverishly stroking her head, talking without knowing what he was saying but begging her to live, not to give in. And the men just watched him, perhaps caring, if only for his grief. They got the injured men out of the cart and then two of them went off on their own to see what help could be found.

After what seemed an age they came back in a lorry and their waiting companions let out cheers and exclamations of disbelief.

'There was a village just over the hill. Our men are there. We'll be all right now.'

Quickly the wounded were lifted into the truck, helped by the militia-men from the village who had brought cans of water which was hurriedly grasped at. They seemed to have forgotten Gaviota until one of them came back and poured some water over her head. She blew through her nostrils, lifted her head a little then laid it back with a sigh.

'You'd better get up front with the driver,' one of them said to Eduardo. 'We'll get you home if we can.'

'And what about Gaviota?'

'There's no point in worrying about her. She's had it. Get in the lorry and we'll do what we can for you.'

'I can't just leave her!' he exclaimed.

'Don't be crazy. She's as good as dead. What can you do for her now?'

'Stay with her, anyway.'

'Put him in the lorry,' someone yelled, 'and let's get going.'

The man grabbed him round the waist and lifted him off his feet. Eduardo lost all reason in that iron grip. He struck out madly, screaming to be released, kicking and pushing against the lorry as he was shoved up over the tail-board. Someone grabbed his legs. There was a hard hand across his face, half suffocating him as he struggled. Instinctively his teeth sunk into it and the next thing he knew light was exploding round him. The heavy blow knocked him backwards into the truck and by the time he came to his senses it was already under way. His head rocked and he could feel all one side of his face puffing up, stinging and burning.

He pulled himself up to look over the tail-board. The road was empty. Gaviota was already out of sight, forgotten by everyone but him. He kept on looking at the road anyway, hands clenched tight on the tail-board, silent tears dropping on to them.

19

The village wasn't very far away. Gaviota had almost made it. If only she could have kept on a little longer she would be here now, resting in someone's stable, and Eduardo would be standing beside her, feeding her barley corn by the handful and bathing her injured knees.

Although he was so hungry he could hardly eat the bowlful of lentils that were pushed under his nose and the slice of potato omelette waiting beside it on the table. All he could think of was Gaviota lying on the road by herself, abandoned after giving all she had to give, dying alone. Was she dead already? For her sake he hoped so. He couldn't bear to think of her lingering on and on through the night, perhaps refusing to die in the belief that he would return to her. The men said she was as good as dead. They ought to know.

While he tarried over the soup, pushing it into his mouth and trying to swallow, forcing himself because he didn't want these men to see him crying and swallowing tears along with the lentils, he remembered how she had begun her life, alone on an icy winter's night, abandoned by her mother who had died. If his Aunt Angeles hadn't gone to look for her, if she hadn't cared enough to want to save her, she would have died then, before she was twenty-four hours old.

'Kept her alive with words and will-power,' Baltasar had said. 'That foal just didn't dare to die.'

And now? Was she too tired to live? Had she given up because no one cared enough to will her into living? He was ashamed of himself as he sat there at the table with the loud-voiced militia-men, eating their food, crying over her but doing nothing for her. But he was so tired, so very tired. All he really wanted was to be with his mother again, and as soon as possible. Now. Now. With nothing to care or worry about, not even Gaviota. He had failed her miserably.

'Why are you crying, boy?' someone asked him, a round-faced fellow with merry eyes.

'I want to be with my mother,' he answered, letting the tears fall wildly now, no longer caring.

'Your mother's a long way away,' someone answered him. Someone must have told them that he was trying to get to Galicia.

'Then I want to be with my horse.'

'Don't worry. We'll find someone to look after you. Forget about the horse. Horses don't matter.'

Eduardo stared at him, seeing only blurred features through his tears. A rebuke burned in his heart but stayed there, not reaching his lips. Horses didn't matter. Even people didn't matter any more. He had a flashing memory of the young man who had been left propped against the tree under which he had given up his suffering, nameless in a bloody uniform. Had they forgotten about him, too?

He was taken to someone's house to sleep but was too numbed with exhaustion and misery to care about the people who gave him shelter. There were other children there who crowded round him and asked him questions, but he was mute and deaf among them and soon he was left on his own in a sour-smelling little bedroom which had but two big mattresses on the floor and sheets made out of flour sacks. He fell asleep almost immediately, without even undressing, and when he awoke it was to find himself in darkness still but surrounded by the sleeping, outstretched bodies of his host's family.

The heat was intense and he could hardly breathe, with a wall at his back and a small body curled up almost into his stomach, its legs tangled with his own. For a while he just lay there, hovering between thoughts and dreams, and a picture of Gaviota came into his head. The proud, magnificent Gaviota, bedecked with plumes and ribbons, tinkling golden bell and sparkling silver and gold flowers. It was only a dream, that picture of Gaviota. The real Gaviota was an old grey mare with a flowing mane the colour of steel who pricked her ears when she saw a tin of barley corn and made funny grunting noises of pleasure whenever he went to see her.

So why did he keep seeing that other picture of her, streamers in her tail, gold on her reins, and Baltasar telling him not to be afraid?

With Baltasar, his memory returned. He wasn't dreaming any more. This muggy little room was real, as were the bodies in the streets of Badajoz, the militia-man sitting for eternity under the tree, Gaviota jerking spasmodically at the roadside, and his heart beat violently as the different memories flashed unbidden into his mind, refusing to leave him alone. Lying there, not even knowing where he was or the names of the people who had taken him in, he felt as though his heart and his head would burst. He had to get out. He couldn't stay there a moment longer.

Carefully he freed himself from his neighbour, who immediately flung his arm across the next boy's cheek. He was lying beneath the window but he couldn't get out that way without knocking all the plant pots into the street. He picked his way over to the door, opened it cautiously and found the rest of the house in darkness. Everyone was asleep. No one was aware of his creeping out, even though he banged his shins against a heavy bench and almost knocked over a wicker chair.

There was air in the street and freedom from his terrible memory pictures and for a while he just stood there, taking in the stars and the bright three-quarter moon, while the whole village slept and all the moon-silvered houses were silent.

There was only one thing Eduardo wanted to do now. It was suddenly as clear to him as the moon riding so high above him. He had to find out if Gaviota was dead – if Gaviota was still alive. He would never be able to forget about her until he knew, and even as he began to trot down the road in her direction an unbidden hope seared within him. Let her be still alive! Don't let her be dead! Let her have more will-power, more courage than he had!

As he hurried along the silent, moonlit road he prayed and made promises, if only Gaviota could still be alive.

The cart came into sight, silhouetted by the high riding moon, no longer sinister-looking without its grisly passengers. Eduardo could see the spokes of the wheels and the one good shaft but there was no dark shape where Gaviota had been. His heart leaped with almost unbearable excitement. If she wasn't still there then she couldn't be dead. She couldn't be dead!

He ran the last fifty metres or so, overcome with incredible joy, and he stood before the cart, looking at the broken shaft, the harness in a jumble where the men had thrown it after dragging it from Gaviota's blistered body, still hardly able to believe his eyes. Then, as he began to look about the countryside, trees showing up plainly against the green-blue sky, even the stiff stalks of grass, he caught a movement somewhere on the very edges of the black shadows of the hills and heard Gaviota's little whicker of greeting as he had heard it so many times before.

'Gaviota,' he yelled and flung himself towards her, careless of the thistles that stung him and roots that caught his feet.

A patch of white, caught by the moon. It was Gaviota, and it was all Eduardo needed. She didn't go forward to meet him; she remained half in the shadows; but those soft little sounds came from her throat and soon he could see her pricked ears and glistening eyes. Then his arms were round her neck, tangled with the reins which hadn't been removed, and he was crying into her jowl, his fingers clutching her mane.

She gave a heavy sigh.

20

When the sun came up most of Eduardo's happiness faded because then he could see only too clearly that, even though Gaviota wasn't dead, she was dying. She hadn't wanted to die by the roadside. Some inner urge had forced her to all fours, made her drag herself to the shadows of this orchard of cork trees, but from here she had no wish to move.

Eduardo carefully removed the bridle from her head and threw it into the dust, hating the metal noseband that had rubbed the skin from her so gentle and sensitive nose, but his hate could only turn to despair when the indifferent sun showed up every wound on her body, from the swollen, bloody knees and broken hooves to the skin rubbed off here and there, wherever the stiff, heavy harness had galled her. She wouldn't move and her head hung low, but while she was still on all fours Eduardo wouldn't give up hope.

He talked to her; oh, how he talked to her, not even knowing what words he used, wanting only for her to understand that she mustn't give in, that somehow – if she hung on – she would be saved.

If only he could find water! Where did the trees get their sustenance, how did the grass and thistles survive? Lizards slipped from rock to rock, ants busy-bodied everywhere. Did none of them need water ever?

Only Gaviota's ears moved from time to time as he spoke to her, and her eyes followed his movements as long as she didn't have to turn her head. But she uttered no more sounds, not even a sigh. She was like a battered grey rock, waiting for time to crumple her.

Eduardo eventually ran out of words. He had said everything. Only silence remained. He couldn't even cry although her patience made him ache. Together they shared the shadows of a cork tree and waited.

A woman came along, dressed in black from head to ankles, a big basket on her left arm. What she was doing tramping across the deserted landscape Eduardo had no idea. She stopped only a short way off, looked at the boy and the horse and at the cart on the roadside, then with sharp, hard tones asked, 'What are you doing here?'

'Nothing. Waiting.'

'Waiting! You'll wait here for ever. What are you waiting for?'

'The horse. I think she's dying. She can't move.'

'Hmm.'

With determined stride the woman walked all round Gaviota, thin lips pursed, black eyes shrewd.

'A fine state she's in! But why are you here, too? Can't she die on her own?'

'No,' said Eduardo. 'She's my friend.'

'Ah!' After a silence she went on, 'Well, if you don't particularly want her to die – I mean, if you'd rather she lived, I've a house over the hill and you'll find water there in a big pitcher. Put some in a bucket and bring it to her. It might do her some good.'

'Will you show me the way?' asked Eduardo, hardly able to believe this good fortune.

'No. I've got work to do, but if you can keep her alive till nightfall, and can get her to my place, I'll see you this evening. It's the only house over the hill, so you can't mistake it. There's no dog to bite you and nothing to steal, so help yourself to the water.' And she was gone, waiting for no reply.

When Eduardo first brought the water, spilling some of it

on the way because the bucket was heavy and he was weak, Gaviota only brushed her lips over it and didn't want to drink. Eduardo cupped his hands and held some up under her nose, seeing the precious, sun-sparkling drops flee through his fingers to disappear almost immediately into the insatiable earth. He splashed it over her nose, rubbed it round her ears and forehead, even tried poking some of it into her stubbornly closed mouth, and it grew warm in the bucket while still she would not drink.

'Please, Gaviota,' he begged her. 'Drink it for me. Even if you don't really want it, drink it for me.'

And she did, but not all at once. For a long time she just stood with her nose almost touching it, hardly even breathing because there was not the slightest ripple on the now dusty surface. Her eyes were shut. She seemed either asleep or in some kind of coma. Eduardo just watched her, oblivious of the sun, the heat, the time. All of a sudden her muzzle hit the water unexpectedly. This action seemed to wake her up and she began to drink with such haste that in only a minute the bucket was empty, except for the drips that fell back from her jaws.

Eduardo ran all the way to the house for a second bucketful. She drank most of this, too, but left some at the bottom which she obviously didn't want. Gratefully Eduardo washed his burning face with it.

The water revived her considerably. She didn't want to eat anything, even though Eduardo tried tempting her with the best-looking grass he could pick and flowers from the thistle tops, but she moved her head and occasionally swished her tail.

Eduardo fell asleep in the shade of the cork tree and when he woke up Gaviota was standing beside him. She had moved at least two metres while he was asleep and so he determined to make her go to the woman's house. It was as if in spite of herself she was indestructible.

It took him a long time to get Gaviota over that one small hill. Every stride required supreme effort on her part and she wasn't very interested in helping herself. Whether it was obedience to the word 'hakma' or fondness for him that made her follow him, Eduardo could not tell. He liked to think it was because there was a bond between them, but so many times did she halt, and with such an expression of weariness in her gaze as if begging him to leave her, that he couldn't tell. He knew instinctively that really she didn't want to go with him. The earth claimed her and she wanted its solitude.

The house, if such it could be called, was a tumbledown adobe ruin, with nothing to steal as the woman had claimed. A mattress, a chair, not even a table. A few cooking utensils, some salt in a jar, and the water. Where that had come from, he didn't know.

Night had fallen before she returned, her basket laden with eggs, a loaf of bread, a few tomatoes and garlic heads and, tied up in a dirty rag, a couple of handfuls of barley corn.

'I stole that,' she said, 'in case you got the horse back. The other things I paid for.'

She gave half her bread to Eduardo, together with a couple of tomatoes and some of the garlic. The eggs would be taken into town early the next morning. Eduardo discovered that this was the woman's livelihood. She roamed the countryside, visiting every house where a few hens were kept, collected the eggs which she sold in the town and for their owners brought back the things they needed, combs, needles, some dried cod or medicines, charging a miserably small commission for her efforts. None of them could afford to eat their own eggs, unless it was for a very special occasion. In one day she would walk perhaps forty kilometres, with just a bit of bread or a head of garlic to sustain her.

All this she explained to Eduardo that first night as they sat on the floor beside her only light, a wick soaked in cooking oil. She was a talkative soul but as soon as their food was gone she went off to her mattress, as she had to be up with the sun the next day, and Eduardo was left to his own devices.

He fed the corn to Gaviota and to his delight she took it. Perhaps she had decided not to die after all. He lay down on the ground beside her, just outside the house, covering himself with an old coat the woman had offered him, but not until he had bathed Gaviota's knees and rubbed some of the lamp oil into her sores.

The next day the woman told Eduardo where to go for water, at a spring several kilometres away, and in the evening she made him help her drag the cart back to her house, an almost impossible feat which they achieved only because she was determined to have it.

'It's too good a thing to leave on the highway. We'll see about mending it one of these days.'

While she was away, Eduardo tended to Gaviota. There was no more corn, after those two handfuls, but he spent hours in the countryside cutting forage for her with the help of a stick because she was too stiff and lame to move very far. He did this every day and at first she ate very poorly, hardly caring for what he offered her, but soon she was taking the thistle flowers from his blistered hands and shaking her head impatiently for more. He began grooming her again, hoping to see a shine return to her dappled skin, but he didn't know what to do about her knees or her broken hooves.

'She needs a farrier to attend to her hooves,' the woman advised him, watching him one day. 'But there's no money for that. Besides, I think the farrier's gone off to the war.'

Eduardo could never have imagined the poverty in which this woman lived. There was never more than bread and a few vegetables to eat, with which she would sometimes make a soup, and yet she had the endurance of the very thistles which blossomed out of nothing. His own previous existence, with two three-course meals a day, servants to wait on him, a daily bath and change of clothes, the Sunday outings with food of every kind in what now seemed dream-like abundance, a balconied room of his own with the most comfortable feather bed and best quality furniture, was something that had no connection with his present world at all. Her talk of children who had died because there was no food to put in their stomachs, of furniture which had to be sold to pay for her husband's funeral, was like something from a book of gruesome fairy tales. And yet she shared what she had with him and had even troubled to bring two handfuls of corn for the horse.

'Anyway,' she added hopefully after one of these doleful stories, 'things will get better now that the villagers have taken over the land. It'll be shared out fairly between us, good with bad, and then a horse like Gaviota will be useful. We shall need to plough this winter. She should be better by then. And we can rent her out to other farmers.'

'She's not a plough horse,' cried Eduardo.

'None of us are but life turns us into plough horses whether we like it or not. We can grow barley for her as well as crops for ourselves.'

Against such determined animation he decided not to argue, knowing only too well that Gaviota was in no condition to be taken away from there. She could hardly walk more than a few paces and her only hope of survival lay in being able to rest for a long time. If the woman turned him away he would have to abandon Gaviota, and he hadn't come back to her for that.

So he stayed on at the lonely house, alone all day except for the mare, and he fed her and talked to her and continued to bathe her inflamed legs, not knowing what else he could do for her, not thinking about the future because it was too unreal to contemplate, knowing, too, that he was afraid to travel the lonely road again after his last experience.

The only real things were his hunger and the sick horse, and he was glad that the woman was away most of the day because he knew now that her friendliness had a price. When she asked him about his family he said very little, realizing that there was a great gulf between them. The villagers had murdered the local land owner, the same way as in another place his father had been murdered, and she was glad and crowed about his death. Eduardo knew he had no right to eat her bread, but his stomach cared nothing for loyalties, so he took it and stayed.

21

After only four days the soldiers came to the village. Eduardo heard about it from the woman when she returned from her daily round. He knew that a battle had taken place somewhere that morning because the noises of it had been carried to him, but it hadn't lasted very long and he had forgotten about it until she began to speak. There was a great bitterness in her eyes which the small light from the oil wick emphasized as she told him how death had exploded among those small white houses, hand grenades and bullets killing children and old people while the young men had been lined up in the square and shot.

'Even those sick militia-men, the ones your horse carried in the cart. They were shot, too,' she said. 'They might just as well have stayed in Badajoz.'

Eduardo said nothing, not wanting to hear about death and suffering, and he took his bit of bread and salt, which was all there was that night, to eat outside, where he could gaze on Gaviota and forget that a world existed beyond the stars, the shadows of the hills, her gentle eyes and questing ears.

The woman was too afraid to set out on her usual rounds the next day. She was also afraid to stay in the house and said it would be best if both of them hid somewhere in the hills until the soldiers had gone.

'They might come here,' she said. 'They're hunting everywhere like savage beasts.'

But Gaviota was unable to follow them and Eduardo, frightened as he was of men in uniform, men of any kind by now, was frightened still more of losing her. The woman didn't bother to argue. Very soon she was out of sight and Eduardo was alone once more.

The morning passed as it always did. He went for water, he went for forage, beating at the dry grasses with his stick and gathering them into a pile for Gaviota. She watched him from the distance, seeming to know what he was up to, her ears pricked with anticipation, blowing with pleasure when he came back to her, his arms laden with the grasses that scratched his skin and made it itch. He stood beside her while she ate, his eyes wandering over every part of her body, trying to assess whether she was improving or not, wondering if she would ever really be well again. At least she was on her feet. As long as she didn't lie down he felt sure she would get better.

Gaviota became aware of the approaching horsemen before he did. She let out a loud whinny of greeting which one of the horses answered, and by the time Eduardo realized that the riders were soldiers they had already seen him and there was no point in hiding from them.

They stopped at some little distance from the house, their animals glistening as once Gaviota had glistened, and one of them held his submachine gun as if prepared for an ambush or some kind of enemy activity from within the tumbledown walls.

'Come here, boy,' commanded his companion and as Eduardo approached, heart beating with fear, he saw that this man, like his Uncle Teodoro, was a lieutenant of the Legion. His gaze was cold, scornful.

'Where did you steal that horse?' he said.

'I didn't steal her. She's mine.'

'Yours! Since when do peasants keep hot-blooded horses instead of mules or donkeys? You've stolen her from some-

where, haven't you – you or your father. Where is he, anyway?'

Tears sprang involuntarily into Eduardo's eyes. For all that he had gone through in the last few weeks, it was still too much for him to have this man, who could have been his uncle if only his face was different, shouting at him, calling him a thief, asking derogatively for his father.

'Perhaps we've already shot him,' he went on, watching Eduardo's desperate tears fall without compassion. 'Speak, boy. Who lives here with you?'

All Eduardo could do was shake his head, tears falling as if they'd never stop, perhaps all the tears he hadn't yet cried for his father.

'Come closer,' demanded the lieutenant and, when he obeyed, he leaned from the saddle to grab him by the shirt collar while pulling a pistol from its holster which he held to Eduardo's head. Then, with a nod, he ordered the sergeant to reconnoitre the house, shouting at the top of his voice, 'If anyone in there makes a false move, this boy dies.'

When the sergeant returned, no longer suspicious, the lieutenant let him go. He dismounted and went to look at Gaviota. He let out an oath at the sight of her broken knees and splintered hooves. 'You people just don't know how to look after a decent animal. Where did you get her from?' he asked again, eyes blazing with anger.

'I told you. She's mine and she wasn't like that before. She was beautiful.'

There was something about his tone, perhaps the fact that it didn't occur to Eduardo to call him sir or react in any servile way in spite of his obvious terror, even his pronunciation, that made the lieutenant believe there might be some truth in Eduardo's story.

'Tell me,' he commanded. 'You're not one of these people are you?' and when Eduardo shook his head, 'Then speak. You've got a tongue, haven't you?'

Where could he begin? What could he say? All of a sudden there was no past in his head, only memories of blood and violence, haggard faces, desperate eyes and Gaviota; Gaviota always with him, the only sane, good thing in his life.

After a long silence the lieutenant asked, 'What's your name? Where do you come from? And your parents, where are they? What are you doing here with this horse?'

The questions went on and on and Eduardo answered them without thinking, without feeling, except that when asked for his father's whereabouts the tears began to fall again and he said he didn't know.

'Well, well,' finished the lieutenant when he had all the information he needed and after writing some of it down in a notebook. Then he said in a gentler tone, 'Do you want to come back to headquarters with us?'

Eduardo violently shook his head. 'I want to stay here with Gaviota.'

The lieutenant looked at the mare. 'The kindest thing for her,' he said, 'would be a bullet through the head.'

'She's going to get better,' Eduardo shouted at him. 'I'm going to make her get better.'

'All right, all right. It was only a suggestion. I'll see if I can send someone along to look at her for you, attend to her legs at least. You'll let me do that, won't you?'

His tone was kinder now. He was talking like a man instead of a soldier and Eduardo nodded hesitatingly, afraid of what he might be conceding. The lieutenant squeezed Eduardo's shoulder and the glimpse of the stars on his sleeve reminded him of someone else.

'I have an uncle in the Legion,' he admitted cautiously.

'You don't stop surprising me, do you, boy?' said the lieutenant, getting out his notebook again. 'Tell me, what's his name and rank? Do you know his rank?'

'He's a lieutenant, like you. Teodoro Caballero.'

The man grinned at him and pretended to punch him on

the chin. 'Well, well. As they say, it's a small world. Anyway,' he continued, remounting his chestnut gelding and nodding to the sergeant, 'you'll be hearing from me soon, so don't go away. As for the mare,' he added, giving her one last rueful stare then shrugging, 'Well, don't give up hope. She's alive, anyway.'

Then the pair of them were gone, pushing their horses into a canter and disappearing over the hill.

22

The woman returned at sunset, her apron full of pomegranates so swollen with seeds that the skins were bursting. Such was their hunger that they ate without words until every skin was bare, with purple juice running down their chins and fingers. The woman let Eduardo have two more than herself.

'You've got to grow,' she said. 'You need more than I do,' and Eduardo accepted them with discomfort, even in his hunger, because he had decided that he couldn't tell her about the lieutenant even if she asked him any questions.

However, she asked him nothing, still brooding over the destruction and slaughter in the village, but she told him that the next day she would have to go back to her egg collecting if they were to survive, regardless of the soldiers.

'If they catch me and decide to kill me,' she argued, 'then at least my troubles will be over. And if they leave me alone, I'll still curse them into their graves.'

The tone of her words made him doubly aware of his treachery – for as such she would see it, as such he saw it himself – but she mistook his expression for one of fear and to comfort him went on briskly, 'Never mind. Tomorrow there'll be bread, I promise you.'

The lieutenant kept his word and sent a horse doctor the very next day to look at Gaviota. Eduardo had hardly dared to hope that anyone would come, so many had been the broken promises, but as soon as the man arrived, accompanied by the sergeant of the day before, he realized that he should have had confidence in the lieutenant's word. The Army of Africa could do anything it set its mind to. Now he knew for certain that his Uncle Teodoro would come too and that soon, perhaps sooner than he could even imagine, he would be reunited with his mother in Galicia.

But for the moment he cared only for what the horse doctor might say about Gaviota, unable to forget the lieutenant's words, 'The kindest thing for her would be a bullet through the head.' He stood beside her and stroked her neck, feeling sick with dread, unable to tell from the man's expression what he thought as he passed knowledgeable hands up and down Gaviota's legs and examined her closely from teeth to rump.

He had had plenty of time to think since yesterday and the biggest question, still unanswered, was what would he do if his uncle came while Gaviota was still too lame to be moved and insisted on taking him home without waiting for her to get better? And could he really take her to Galicia, anyway? On the road, when there were just the two of them, everything had seemed possible but now, with adults taking charge again, he knew he would have to do whatever they decided for him.

In the last few weeks he had faced too much reality to be able to deceive himself now. He knew he was going home and he knew, even before the horse doctor spoke, that he would be going home without Gaviota. Yesterday, after the lieutenant had gone, he had tried to make her walk; tried to convince himself that she could do it if both of them wanted it badly enough; but her obvious pain and stubborn refusal, as if she knew her own limitations far better than he did, made him accept the crushing of his last illusion.

Gaviota was old and lame and sick and a long way from anyone who would care for her once he was gone. His dread was not that the horse doctor should confirm his knowledge;

his dread was having to find the courage to agree to her destruction.

'Is this animal yours?' the horse doctor asked him when he'd finished his examination. 'I mean, is there anyone else responsible for her apart from yourself?'

Eduardo shook his head, heart beating fast, anticipating the words that would condemn her.

'The tendons are badly sprained. She must be feeling a lot of pain. A great deal of care and attention are needed if she's to get better. Even then – '

'You mean, she will get better? She won't have to die?' he interrupted impatiently.

'That's not what I said. She's been a good mare but those legs will never carry more than her own weight again and not even that always.'

'How long does she need to get better?' If his uncle could wait a week or so . . .

'I could fire the tendons but it'd be months before she was fit. If a quick decision has to be made, the best thing would be to have her put down.'

'And if you didn't – didn't fire her, what would happen to her? Would she die?'

'She'd keep breaking down. She'd often be in pain but she wouldn't die – at least, not as a direct result of her lameness.'

Eduardo looked at Gaviota, not wanting to meet the man's gaze, knowing he was waiting for him to make up his mind. She looked so decrepit; the shine all gone from her, her stance as she tried to keep the weight off her forequarters giving a cruel shape to the whole of her weary body; it was painful to recall his memory of her in plumes and gold. If he left her here perhaps the woman would make her plough the land even though she was lame, making her work until she dropped, driven as the militia-men by desperate need. Wouldn't death be preferable to that?

The mare's eyes met his own, dark and unknowing, full

of trust in him. How could he possibly take away the life that was in them?

'When my uncle comes,' he said at last, 'he'll be able to decide.'

'I might not be able to come back. I shouldn't really be here at all. If you don't want her put down, I can fire the legs anyway. The sergeant will help me. Anyone can shoot her afterwards, if you change your mind.'

'Will it be painful?'

The man shrugged. 'Having a tooth out can be painful but you feel a lot better when it's done.'

'But what do you have to do to her?'

The man turned back to Gaviota, pointing to the swollen parts above her knees, demonstrating with his hands as he explained, 'I burn her with an iron, here and here. The tendons have been overstretched, you see. Firing makes them shrink, the same as a piece of meat shrinks when you cook it. It tightens them up and makes a kind of permanent bandage. There's really nothing else that can put any strength back into her legs.'

With the help of the sergeant Eduardo gathered fuel for a fire. A tremendous amount was needed to produce a bed of ashes both thick and hot enough for the horse doctor's requirements. Every now and then he inspected the irons as they began to glow, and whenever he did this Eduardo turned his head away, fiercely having to remind himself that it was for Gaviota's good.

From his bag the horse doctor produced both a blindfold and a twitch. Gaviota was already growing nervous, as if able to sense that some kind of attack was about to be made upon her, but the blindfold immediately silenced her snorts and blowing even though she trembled and began to sweat.

Then, at a word from the horse doctor, the sergeant put the twitch round her muzzle and tightened it until it would turn no more.

'You keep out of the way, boy,' the horse doctor shouted at Eduardo. 'She'll probably kick like the very devil in spite of it all.' And he was glad of an excuse for running away without seeming a coward, already shaken just by the preparations.

When he came back, when it was over, Gaviota seemed calmer than he was. The horse doctor was stroking her neck and saying soothing things to her. Eduardo's throat was too dry for words.

'There's some corn for her in the sergeant's saddle-bags,' he said when he saw him. 'The lieutenant sent it for her, but don't give it to her just yet. Wait till she's stopped sweating.'

He gave him some ointment with directions for its use before going away and in farewell said, 'If I can come back to see how she's getting on, I will. Meanwhile, good luck to you both.'

Along with the corn, the sergeant left him a loaf of bread and a short string of sausages. 'These are from me,' he explained. 'I thought you might need them,' and he brushed away Eduardo's thanks with an embarrassed air.

He saved all the food for the evening, in spite of hungry temptation, glad to have something to offer the woman in his turn despite the difficulty he would have in explaining where it had come from. But when she saw his food and learned how he had come by it, she thrust it away with a cry of contempt.

'You eat it. I'd choke on it.'

He pleaded with her. He wanted her to understand that he hadn't intended to deceive her. He wanted to give her something in return for all she had given him but she was adamant and scornful and, because he persisted, she eventually thrust him out of the room.

'Go and eat with your horse,' she said, 'and leave me in peace.'

Normally she went straight to her mattress when she had finished eating but that night she sat outside under the stars, looking at the unpromising earth on every side, and sighed out loud for what she had nearly had, for what would now never be hers. She cursed the soldiers and all the people who had started the war, using expressions of such deep hatred that Eduardo began to feel afraid and kept out of her sight.

'So. You'll be leaving me soon and when you go you'll take the horse and the cart and the harness, no doubt,' she said to him the next morning as she was about to set out once more.

'Please stay. The lieutenant might come back today. He's not bad. He's not going to hurt you,' Eduardo tried to persuade her. 'Or perhaps my uncle will come. He'll want to give you his thanks for looking after me. Please don't go.'

'These things have nothing to do with me. I'll say goodbye in case you're not here when I come back,' and she marched off with bitterness in her eyes and on her lips, ignorant of the pain in Eduardo's heart. He didn't want her to hate him.

The lieutenant came again in the late afternoon, his expression harder than Eduardo had expected to see it. He examined Gaviota's legs and general appearance and asked a few questions about her before saying, 'Well, there's both good news and bad for you. Which do you want to hear first?'

Eduardo's heart began to beat faster. Surely nothing could go wrong now? Surely his mother was all right and was expecting him home?

'I prefer the good news first,' he almost whispered.

'We've been in touch with your mother. She knows you're all right and she's crazy with joy. She can't wait to see you. It's been arranged for you to be driven up there tomorrow. We have a safe route between here and the north.'

Eduardo could hardly believe what he heard, even though he had been expecting such news. Suddenly everything seemed far too easy.

'I suppose the bad news is about Gaviota?' he said, tightening his features as he looked at the lieutenant, determined to be brave whatever he was about to hear.

'No. It's about your uncle. He was badly wounded at Mérida. He died three days ago. I didn't know myself until yesterday. I'm sorry. He was a friend of mine.'

It was difficult to imagine his Uncle Teodoro being any less alive than this proud-looking man standing before him now, so strong was his last memory of him. He could think of nothing to say.

'The news about the mare is good,' the lieutenant went on, breaking the uncomfortable silence between them. 'We were also able to get in contact with your uncle in Sevilla. He was astonished to hear about all your adventures with her and that she's still alive – that you're both still alive. He says he'll take charge of her and have her returned to his estate just as soon as she's well enough to be moved.'

'Did he say anything about – anything about my father?'

'I wasn't told if he did.'

Eduardo was silent. It was still difficult to accept that his nightmare was over, that tomorrow he would be home, that Gaviota would be taken care of. Could all this possibly be only a dream? He hardly dared speak again in case everything suddenly fell apart.

The lieutenant looked about, at the adobe house half in ruins, set in a landscape of rock-strewn ground, hard and unyielding; and at Gaviota watching him curiously, as much a ruin in his eyes as the walls behind her, hope enduring where no hope should be.

'You'd better say good-bye to all this,' he told Eduardo, 'and to your horse. We'll see that she's well looked after.'

This was the hardest part, saying good-bye to Gaviota, wondering if he would ever see her again, not wanting to leave her but having to. How did you say good-bye to a horse? Once he had wondered how anyone could think of saying anything to a horse, beyond giving it orders to move or stay, and Baltasar had laughed at his ignorance. Baltasar could have taught him a great deal but even he couldn't have told him how to say good-bye to her.

In the end he just stroked her neck, told her to be good and have patience, and then he said to the lieutenant, 'I'm ready.'

23

The war didn't end for nearly three more years, but it ended for Eduardo that afternoon, when the lieutenant took him back to the lines that had been established just beyond the village and he had his first proper meal for days and even a decent bed to sleep in. He didn't sleep much, his stomach heavy with the now unaccustomed amount he had eaten, his heart heavy for Gaviota.

He wondered if she would be missing him. He had slept close beside her for weeks. He wondered if the soldier who had been commissioned to look after her would treat her with kindness and how the woman would react to this invasion of her home. How much more could she possibly be hurt?

And then his mind would jump to his homecoming and he could imagine himself being crushed in his mother's arms as she covered him with tears and kisses, and even while he longed for all this there was a tight pain in his heart because there would be as much sorrow as happiness. His father had promised to take him to Galicia for the summer. The summer was half gone. He didn't even know if his mother knew that his father was dead. And did she know about Uncle Teodoro? With such thoughts there was as much dread as longing for the morrow to arrive.

It was much as he had guessed. The tears, the hugs. Only it shocked him to see his mother dressed in black because she had always worn such light, pretty colours and he almost didn't recognize her. But at least she knew. He didn't have to tell her, which was what he had most been dreading. Then the rest of the family hugged and cried over him, the grandparents, the maiden aunts, the married ones. Then the servants and the neighbours. His cousins stared at him without knowing what to say while all the adults asked ceaseless questions without worrying too much about the answers, which was just as well because Eduardo had nothing to say to any of them.

His mother bathed him, washed his hair and cleaned his fingernails, kissing the cuts and bruises wherever she found them, scrubbing away the smell of horse and earth which he hadn't even noticed and covering him with eau-de-cologne before putting him into bed. He was glad when at last she had left him alone, because for a reason he couldn't understand there was so much pain in his heart. Everyone seemed a stranger to him, even his own mother. He couldn't understand just then that he was seeing them all with different eyes.

The next day she had a doctor examine him from head to toe who, much to her amazement and disbelief, proclaimed him the healthiest boy he had seen for months; then she told him to forget all his nasty experiences, without ever knowing, really knowing, what any of them had been.

He never did tell her very much about his adventures of that July and August, and she wasn't interested in Gaviota. There was no way of making her understand what the mare had meant to him. Once she exclaimed, 'I thought I'd never get rid of that dirty animal smell you came home with!'

Everybody spoke with hatred and scorn of the people who opposed the Nationalist forces although here there was no sign of war. There was plenty of food as always and nothing to fear. All the bad people had been put in prison or executed before they could do anyone any harm.

'And what about those who killed my father?' he had asked.

'Not one of them was left alive,' came his mother's answer hotly. 'Your Uncle Ramon made sure of that.'

At last he learned what had happened to his father after he had gone away, leaving him with his homework and a promise to return. He had stayed at his brother's house overnight and had heard with him on the radio the following morning of the uprising of the officers in Africa. Ramon had immediately decided that his family must be removed to their house in Sevilla, and because his car wasn't big enough for them all, Eduardo's father had agreed to help him, certain that within a couple of hours he could be back at his own house, collect his son and make straight for Galicia before very much would start to happen on the mainland. But somewhere on the road back between the two villages he had been stopped and murdered, and no one had known anything about it until the soldiers arrived to impose their own order and make reprisals.

Less than eight weeks earlier Eduardo himself had burned for revenge against the villagers, but now there was no satisfaction in knowing they were dead. Instead of being jubilant he felt like crying. For him there were too many dead people and he no longer knew who were good and who were bad. Cándido and Baltasar, Maruja and Hortensia, the woman who had shared her hunger and her hovel with him, the lieutenant, the militia-men, the gypsies – of them all only the gypsies had really been bad because they had deceived him, and they had had nothing to do with the war at all. But he said nothing to his mother or anyone else, sure they would never understand. Even he didn't really understand.

A long time went by before he heard any news of Gaviota. A letter came from his Uncle Ramon, telling him how as soon as she had been capable of walking she had been removed to the village, where she was stabled at the civil guard barracks and treated like a queen. There she had spent six months, carefully exercised to bring the strength back to her legs and with a diet sheet as complicated as a book of arithmetic, his uncle said. Now she was back at the estate, hanging round the house as she had always done in the past, being a nuisance sometimes because she was so full of herself, more like a two-year-old filly than an old mare. There was a boy looking after her to whom she had taken quite well, but she didn't follow him about as she had Angeles and Baltasar.

'Fancy writing so much about a horse,' his mother complained. 'He hardly says a thing about anything else. Still, that's typical of him I suppose.'

Eduardo didn't tell her it was the only thing he wanted to know. His mother answered the letter but he didn't add anything to it. He couldn't send a message to Gaviota, after all, and although he had reason to be grateful to his uncle for caring so much about her, all the admiration and friendliness he had once felt towards him had gone.

About a year after that his uncle wrote again to say that Gaviota had given birth to a chestnut colt-foal, twice as beautiful as Azabache and with a look that assured he would be ten times as intelligent.

'She's an incredible mare,' he wrote. 'One day, when the war is over, you must come and see her.' He mentioned also that his two eldest sons were now soldiers, fighting near Madrid.

The war had ended by the time Gaviota's next foal was born, this time a grey like herself and a filly.

'A princess,' enthused Ramon, 'and that's what I'm going to call her. You can't imagine how grateful I am that you saved Gaviota for me,' the letter went on. 'The best horses had gone by the time I was able to return home. As for the bulls – the less said about them the better. I am a broken man. However, with Gaviota, as well as a couple of other mares that have survived, and a stallion on lease from the army, I hope to be able to build up a new Andalusian strain. I wouldn't have had the heart to start again if it hadn't been for Gaviota. She's all we have left from the old times, and the best at that.'

For a little while Eduardo longed for the opportunity to go and see this new little creature, remembering Baltasar's story of Gaviota's birth and having with this foal the chance to know what she must have looked like, but travelling was still very complicated, his mother was dead against it and besides, there were exams to study for and he didn't really have the time to spare. But his heart beat fast for a moment while he thought of it.

He hadn't touched or spoken to a horse since those days with Gaviota. He wondered if he ever would again.

Spain 1936

Churches burned to ground	160
Political murders	269
Assaults	1287
Political centres wrecked	69
Newspaper offices wrecked	10
General strikes	113
Partial strikes	228

In July

The Army of Africa was Spain's only professional corps, maintained for the country's defence. It was composed of two forces, the Foreign Legion and the Moorish 'Regulares', both commanded by Spanish officers and with a reputation for extreme violence and fearlessness. With Spain in total anarchy, many officers believed that their oath to defend the country from 'enemies within and without' was more important than their oath of allegiance to the government of the day.

On the 17th of July officers of the Army of Africa mutinied, and the next day a state of war was officially declared against the Republic. This act of rebellion was the culmination of a hundred and thirty years of violent and passionate quarrels and heralded Spain's last summer of freedom for nearly forty years.